I0760469

FANTASY & FAIRYTALES
BOOK ONE

GOLDEN CURSE

M. LYNN

Edited by Melissa A. Craven
Proofread by Patrick Hodges
Cover design by Covers by Combs
Interior design by Bookly Style

ISBN : 978-1-970052-66-4 (Hardcover)
ISBN-13: 978-1983371813 (Paperback)
ASIN: B07HYP46DH (ebook)

Also by M. Lynn

The Fantasy and Fairytales series

The True Story of Rapunzel

Golden Curse
Golden Chains
Golden Crown

The True Story of Cinderella

Glass Kingdom
Glass Princess

The True Story of Robin Hood

Noble Thief

The True Story of Sleeping Beauty

Cursed Beauty

THE SIX KINGDOMS
DRAGON
GAULE
MADRA
MER
BELA
ANDES
CANA

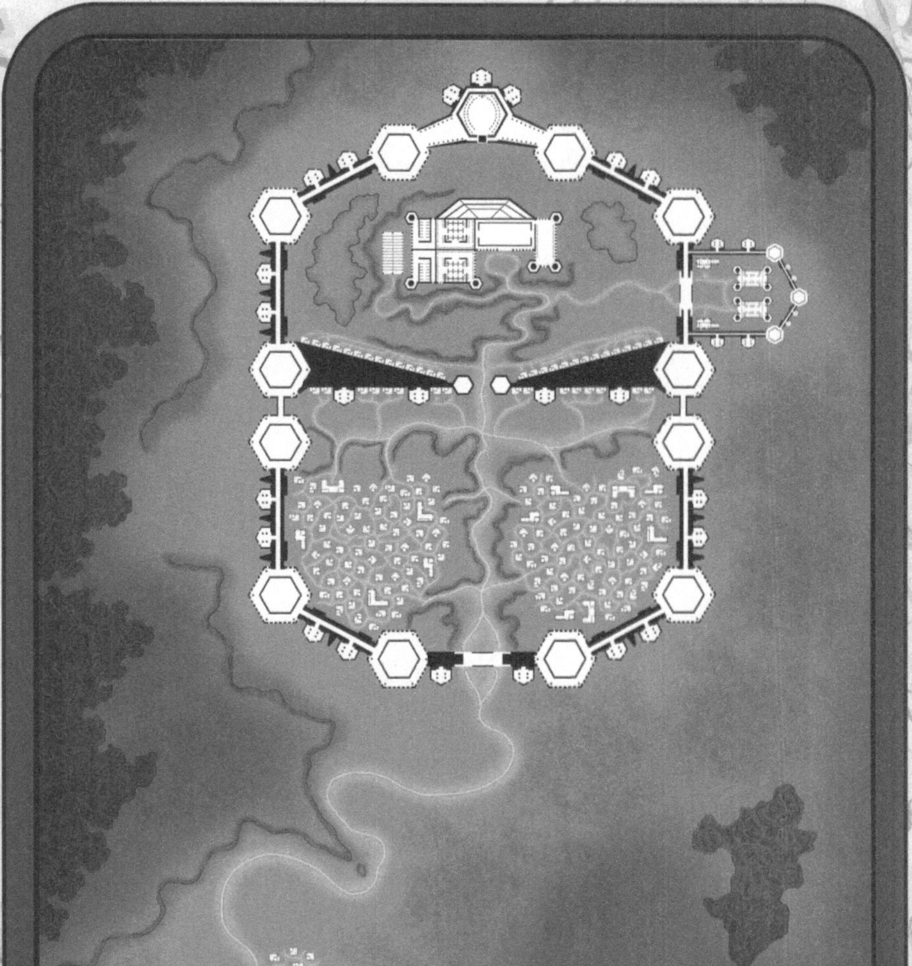

PALACE OF GAULE

For Evelyn

One day when you no longer remember your four-year-old love for princesses, I will. Your wonder makes me believe in the power of stories all over again.

This one is yours, kid, for giving me... everything.

CHAPTER 1

Magic was evil.

That's what they'd been told when it was scrubbed clean from the face of Gaule. Alexandre Durand's father-the king-made sure it couldn't hurt them any longer.

"Brother," Camille said sharply from her spot in the doorway. She stood as proof of magic's cruelty with her twisted leg. Magic folk did that to her the night the purge began.

Alex tuned her out and listened to his lead scraping against paper as an image began to form bright and hopeful. It represented everything the prince could want. He scrunched his face in concentration to apply the final strokes of the magnificent landscape.

It wasn't the palace or the lands surrounding it. When he was a boy, he'd taken a trip across the border into the outer edges of Bela, the forgotten kingdom. The beauty he'd seen there stayed with him. He knew it wasn't real. A friend of his created it. Her magic could make whole fields of flowers bloom.

Not anymore. She was most likely dead. He hated her magic for making her an enemy of Gaule. Persinette. His childhood friend. All he could do as she fled the palace was watch.

He shook his head to rid himself of the thought. Magic was a plague on their land. It was eradicated with good reason.

He set his drawing aside face down, not wanting his sister to see the things he yearned for. He was always on guard around her, lest she report him to their father. She was his favorite little pet.

"What?" he snapped. Exhaustion made him short and dealing with his sister was never easy.

She held up her hands, palms facing him. "I'm just the messenger. You're summoned to the throne room."

"Of course I am." He let out a low growl and ran a hand through his long jet-black hair, tying it back as he did.

His sister watched him with the eyes of a hawk.

He stood and smoothed his tunic before shrugging on his jacket over his surcoat and fastening the gold buttons. It was too warm for the jacket, but his father would know if a single thing was out of place.

He didn't say another word to Camille as he brushed by her and marched down the hall. Velvet carpet muffled his steps while servants and guards ducked out of his way.

The sound of Camille's cane echoed behind him as she struggled to catch up. Guilt twisted his gut, and he slowed. Camille brushed by him without a word.

His fists clenched at his sides and he let out a long breath as he pushed the doors to the throne room open and stepped inside. The opulence soothed him. It always had.

Gaule was doing well with their closed off borders. Without a war to keep them busy, the army had spent years rebuilding roads and cultivating farmland to make the kingdom self-sufficient. They didn't need the rest of the world. Not with the dangers out there.

Servants bustled by, some catching his eye as he stood at the back of the hall, waiting to be called forward.

His brother strode up beside him.

"Where have you been?" Alex asked. Tyson had slipped his guards two days before and no one had seen him since.

The teenage prince laughed and Alex envied his careless freedom. His brother had been too young to be affected by the events of their past. He'd only known peace and prosperity.

"Should I have even asked?" Alex matched his grin.

"Promise not to tell Father?"

"Do I look like Camille?" He glanced to the side to make sure she wasn't near. She'd found some ladies and joined them.

"Fair point. Some friends and I found a tunnel from the palace that goes all the way to the sea."

Alex stopped walking and turned to his brother. "The sea is past the wards."

"Only just. We didn't go through them ... yet." Tyson shrugged.

"Ty, you are not to go there again."

"Wow, way to sound like Father."

Tyson's words stung, but Alex only shook his head. A serving girl stopped in front of them.

"Sires." She dipped into a curtsy.

Alex shifted as she scanned him from head to toe without a word.

"Louisa." Tyson stepped forward and took her hand to place a light kiss on the back. "It is always a pleasure to see you."

Amusement lit in her eyes. She had the grace not to laugh at the prince who was at least ten years her junior. "Thank you, your Highness. I must get on with my duties."

She left and Tyson elbowed his brother in the ribs. "You're too shy, brother."

"I'm a prince. It isn't for me to dally with servants."

Tyson barked a laugh. "Alex, you're a prince, you can dally with whoever you'd like. And I thought you liked blondes."

Alex gasped as if greatly offended. “I can’t believe you would think I’d discriminate.”

Tyson’s laugh bounced across the room, garnering stares from more than a few people. “Good on you, brother. You’re an equal opportunity slag.”

Alex threw his arm around his brother’s neck and locked it there. “I am not having this conversation.”

Tyson tried to wrestle out of Alex’s grip and failed. “You are too predictable.”

Alex released him with a friendly shove. "And you're not? Disappearing for days. Again."

"Being that no one could find me.” Tyson grinned. “I don't think I'm predictable at all." He pushed Alex back.

Their father stood abruptly. “It would be nice if the two princes of Gaule could stand in the throne room without acting like idiots.”

“He means acting like normal people,” Tyson whispered-hissed.

Alex jabbed him with his elbow. “Now would be the time to shut up.”

Their father nodded, and they strode forward, stopping in front of the golden throne. A throne that would one day belong to Alex. Every time he saw it, a chill ran the length of his spine. Some said La Dame crafted it herself. She'd been their ally once, before distrust of magic became the law of the land.

Tall pillars of wood lined the red velvet carpet, creating a path to the king. Their mother was nowhere to be found, but she typically opted out of standing by the king's side.

The king regarded his sons coolly before a smile spread across his face. "My boys," he boomed. "We are to have a tournament!"

Alex straightened and Tyson let out an excited gasp. They loved tournaments. The knights. The swordplay. Alex couldn't help but hope he'd be allowed to participate this time.

"Father, I would be honored to fight for the glory of the crown." Alex kneeled and yanked Tyson down with him.

The king scowled. "Not that kind of tournament."

Alex's heart crashed.

"It is time we find you a protector. Every king has their oathman." He didn't mention that the man who'd once sworn an oath to him had to flee from the palace to avoid being murdered for his magic.

Hearing the title woke something in Alex. Tradition was important to the Durands and to the kingdom.

Tyson laughed and his father glared at him.

"What is funny?" the king snapped.

"It's about time you got someone to protect this oaf." He gestured to Alex. "He's shit with a sword and you won't win many battles if all you can do is shoot an arrow." His grin stretched across his face. "Maybe he should have been a hunter instead of a prince."

His father's expression darkened and Alex wanted to tell his brother to shut the hell up, but before he could, the king rose.

"You're a fool, Son. Do you know our history at all?" He trapped everyone in the room in an attentive trance.

Tyson's smile finally slipped.

"The role of a protector is purely symbolic. As long as Gaule's wards are in place and La Dame cannot cross the border, there will be no need for them to fight for you. They are to provide the appearance of protection and if need be, a sacrifice. Their life is only worth something if you are alive. They will take an arrow for you. They will face death. Your protector is your shadow, your right-hand man. They are an icon of strength."

The thought came unbidden to his mind that Viktor, his father's champion, had been much more than a symbol for many years. Alex got to his feet. He would never betray those loyal to him as his father had, and it was time he had people of his own he could trust.

"Tell me," Alex said.

"Notices have been put up in every village in Gaule. Any fighter can compete in the melee."

"How do you know the winner will be loyal to the crown?"

"Because if they're not, they would not face their ends to be at your side."

"Their ends?" He swallowed hard.

The king nodded. "The tournament will be a battle… to the death."

CHAPTER 2

"I thought we'd agreed you wouldn't use your magic," Viktor Basile growled as he sliced through the vines spreading rapidly across the forest floor.

Etta circled him. "You've said yourself that the people we'll have to fight won't be playing by the rules. Why should I?"

His hand shot out, and he grabbed a fistful of her shirt. "Carelessness will get you killed." He released her and she stumbled back. "You're soon going to take a place inside the palace of Gaule where magic will tie the noose. Don't forget that."

"How could I forget my life is not my own?"

His voice hardened on his next words as he took up his fighting stance again. "If La Dame comes for you, are you going to hesitate? Are you going to fall back and let her take everything you have? Everything you are?"

Etta let the vines still and dodged the path of her father's staff. "No."

"What?" he yelled.

"No!"

The sorceress who'd controlled her family for generations wouldn't have her.

"La Dame won't control me," she growled.

Her father shook his head, regret flashing in his eyes. "Then you have already lost, my daughter. Because she does control you. She does own you. She already has everything you are. That's what it means to be cursed."

"We can fight back."

"No. That's the point. You cannot fight her. If you do, she will own your death as well. I must prepare you to take up the curse and the hardest part is learning not to fight it. Learning to accept that we must serve our enemies."

He came at her again.

Hate. It drove her, begging to be released on her opponent as she jumped, using the toe of her boot to kick off a tree. Only after she spun and landed in a defensive crouch did she raise her eyes once again to her father. No. She couldn't unleash her hate on him no matter the words that left his mouth or the burning inside of her they caused.

She should have seen it coming, but her eyes were so focused on her his blazing stare that she didn't notice his arm jerk to the side seconds before the staff snapped against her back. She crumpled to the ground face first, groaning into the dirt.

"Get up." Viktor Basile's voice was hard, commanding. The voice of a man who was once the crown's protector.

Persinette shifted her hands beneath her chest and pushed up. It wasn't pain or exhaustion that slowed her movements, only annoyance.

Her father clucked his tongue. She glared at him, knowing she could beat him if he didn't rely on petty tricks.

"Etta," he barked. "Stance."

She bent to retrieve her staff and felt the air move to make way for another surprise strike. Spinning out of the way, she twirled her staff and closed her eyes to listen with her magic to the sounds in the earth. Each attempted blow followed a tiny whistling as the wood sailed through the air. Each shift of feet accompanied a change in the earth.

He jabbed at her legs and she jumped, catching her father's weapon between her feet on the way down. His hands lost their grip on it and looked to the ground.

The grass grew over his worn boots. Etta grinned as he tried to break free. They held him firmly in place.

"You have your tricks, Father. I have mine." She jabbed his chest lightly. "Do you concede?"

"Pull your magic back, Persinette." His face reddened.

She stepped back to lean against a tree with her arms crossed over her chest.

The silence between them was almost as vast as the forest surrounding them. The Black Forrest struck fear in the hearts of many people. They believed a danger lurked among the trees. Magic. Evil. For Etta, the danger sat in the castle beyond the Northern edge of the woods.

Finally, her father spoke in his low, dangerous way. "Because using magic will get you killed."

"You say that, but they do not dare come for us here."

He took a knife from the leather sheath on his belt and bent to cut the grasses entombing his feet. When he was finally free, he looked up at her once more. "Soon you won't have the protection of the legends." He started to walk toward the one-room cabin they called home.

She ran after him. "I don't need legends to protect me."

He spun, and she stopped to avoid running into him. "From the crown, maybe. But what about when *she* comes for you?"

"La Dame can't cross the wards as long as magic runs in her blood."

He shook his head. "Have I taught you nothing? You can't rely on forever. Magic does not stretch into eternity. Those wards may not always protect you."

"Then I will fight her. I am a Basile. It's what I'm supposed to do."

"And La Dame is a queen!" His shriek scared a bird from a tree and in the stillness that followed, the flap of its wings were deafening. He breathed out slowly, gathering his control like it was an unraveled rope. "She has ruled Dracon for generations. She can't be destroyed. Her power is unmatched." He put a hand on Etta's shoulder. "Enemies are everywhere, my precious girl. The time for me to protect you is almost past. The best you can do now is follow the path that lies before you. La Dame holds the strings and our family has danced to her rhythm for years. It has been many generations since she destroyed our ancestors and created our curse."

He turned and began walking again. Without looking back, he called, "I'm heading to town for some supplies. You are not to leave these woods. Not like last time."

Etta shivered. Last time she'd journeyed to the market of Gaule, she'd been caught stealing. Two burly men carrying jagged axes had chased her all the way to the edge of the woods. They hadn't dared to follow her into the trees though. No one did.

La Dame would. Etta doubted anything frightened the sorceress queen of Dracon.

The Black Forrest was said to be haunted. Those were the legends Etta's father claimed protected her. The few townsfolk brave enough to venture into the woods, returned with reports of strange sounds—when they returned at all. The forest held many secrets. Chief among them pertained to the last remaining magic in the kingdom. When the great army came all those years ago to destroy any who possessed it, the woods and the protection of her father's wards there had been the only place for many of the magic folk to go.

Her father had shielding magic. The magic he wielded allowed him to craft strong wards to keep people safe, to keep a kingdom safe. That gave him power and made him valuable to the king. And it was why the king tried to kill him. He just hadn't realized killing him would have brought down the wards surrounding Gaule. Wards that kept magic folk both in and out of the kingdom since none could cross the border.

Etta strolled to the river until her pace grew steady and she began to run. The warm summer wind brushed against her cheeks, lifting her long, braided hair off the back of her neck. The clearing came into view and a grin stretched across her face as the sight before her became clear. Vérité stood on the bank with his head dipped low and his mane covering his eyes as he drank.

"Looks like I'm not the only one who could use a wash." She scrunched up her nose and waited for the beast to react to her presence.

He let out a short snort and continued to drink.

Shaking her head, Etta loosened the ties of the armor at her throat. She struggled to pull the thick leather off her sweat-coated skin and over her head.

Vérité picked up his head and his brown eyes met hers. She would've sworn there was amusement in them.

"Yeah?" she said. "I'd like to see you fighting in leather in the heat of the day."

He struck his hoof against the ground and she narrowed her eyes. He was mocking her. Wooden-headed beast.

When the winter freezes came, she'd go a month or more without bathing, even with the constant training that coated her in grime. In those months, she didn't smell much better than Vérité.

But in the summer, she could escape to the river daily. There wasn't enough soap for the ritual, but the water washed away much of the day's filth.

She removed the rest of her clothes and unbraided her hair. It fell down her back in waves. Her fingers dug in, separating the strands. Sometimes, when all it seemed like she'd ever do was train and fight, her hair grounded her. It reminded her she was a woman. It calmed her and made her feel human in a world where they were treated as less than human.

Etta took one more look at Vérité before leaping into the water and let herself sink for a moment before giving a strong kick and breaking the surface. The water hugged her as she floated and flicked it at the horse. He shook his head violently, and she laughed.

Training was hard, but she knew her father was preparing her to take up the family curse, and to be able to protect herself from the enemy she'd serve. He was trying to find a way to get her into the palace household. Soon, the curse would tie her to the Gaulean prince. She was losing time before she'd have to spend her life protecting him.

There were few women in the guard and none so young. Soon, she'd begin feeling the curse tighten around her like unwelcome bonds, only to be loosened when she was in the presence of the one she was destined to serve.

A sigh left her lips. No one had charge of their own fate, but few had theirs set in stone generations before they were even born.

Etta rubbed at her skin until it reddened, wanting to remove all memories of the day. Her father had beaten her too many times. She was better than that. If they'd been sparring with knives instead of poles, he wouldn't have stood a chance.

She stepped from the water and climbed up the bank, wringing out her hair as she went. It had gotten long again, reaching past her waist, but sometimes it was the only thing that made her feel like a real person. Every time her father made her cut it short, she lost a part of herself. The women in town didn't wear their hair short.

It wasn't the first time she realized her father should have had a son. She was the first female forced to take up the curse since it was laid on her ancestors.

She pulled her clothes on over her damp skin and stood beside Vérité. "Feel like a ride?"

Vérité lowered his nose to her shoulder and nudged.

She laughed. Gripping a handful of his mane, she hauled herself onto his bare back. He knew exactly what she wanted without direction. They galloped through the woods. They passed a few houses, and she waved at the magic folk she saw. The people of the forest mostly kept to themselves in the years since escaping among the trees.

Etta closed her eyes, trusting the horse. She remembered that night that brought them here. Eight years ago. The night they'd been forced to flee the castle and run for their lives. The night her mother died. She shook her head and opened her eyes as Vérité slowed. They'd arrived at their favorite place. Every time her father went to town, she escaped to this tapestry of flowers laid out before her. Reds and yellows and blues dotted the landscape as far as she could see.

If outsiders knew the kind of gems the Black Forest offered, they'd never fear it. They'd want it for themselves. Outside people were selfish. She'd seen it first-hand. People living in the streets with no one to help them. Children without families. Armies who would hunt down anyone blessed with the gift of magic.

But the thing only Vérité knew was Etta made this place. While the king called her power evil, she made flowers bloom. While he was only death, she was life.

Yet the hate she held for them filled her with emptiness. The magnificence of this place had no effect on her because even as her magic begged for beauty, she trained for darkness.

She patted Vérité's neck and slid down. "The first born of every generation will be given to the enemy to be their protector. In the shadows or in the light, they will serve day and night." She looked into the wide, chocolate eyes of the beast beside her. "In seven nights I'll be eighteen, my friend, and I must find a way to fulfill the edict of the curse. Only then shall I discover its destruction."

He snorted as if he understood and she sat down among the flowers, drawing warmth from the air into her frozen heart.

Young Etta perched atop the outer wall of the palace, lost in the sounds of daily life. Her father hadn't been home in days and she was anxious to see him ride through the gates. He rarely left the king's side and that meant many journeys throughout the kingdom.

She's gotten in trouble in lessons for telling stories of La Dame.

To most of the children, the sorceress was nothing more than a dark figure used to scare the children. Yet none of them knew the things Etta understood. That La Dame would come for them. She was the most powerful woman in the world, not a simple bedtime story.

But none of the other children had magic. They hadn't grown up with the legends of Bela as they were forbidden in most households of Gaule.

Etta scanned the streets of the outer castle.

She stood from her crouch and ran along the wall. Her mother would be furious if she saw. Arms flung out to her sides, Etta balanced perfectly, pride puffing out her chest as she looked down on the rooftops along the wall. Small houses lined the outer edges of the castle.

The jangling and stomping of many armored boots sounded against the cobblestone street below and she froze, trying to think if she'd stolen anything in the past few days. No. They couldn't be there for her. She peered down as they yanked a man from his house along the wall. His nightgown clung to his legs as the soldiers hauled him further from his waiting bed. Terrified wailing sounded from inside the house and Etta couldn't take it any longer. She ran the length of the wall and jumped onto the corner roof that belonged to her family.

Sliding down the angled tiles, she gripped the edge and jumped down onto the crates that held their chickens.

A loaded wagon sat by the door.

Father must be home. He'd want to hear what she'd just seen.

The wooden front door swung open on rusted hinges and Etta stopped moving, her mouth hanging open. A metallic scent hung in the air, so thick she could taste it. A guard stood near the roaring fire, warming his blood-soaked hands. Waiting. Just waiting.

Etta silently scanned the room, immediately finding the deep red blood as it soaked into the wooden floorboards. It moved and swirled like it was a living thing. But how could it be living when the woman it came from was so obviously dead?

The body on the floor couldn't have been her mother. She didn't have her mother's kind smile. The iciness in her eyes wasn't right. The woman had been the warmth in their house.

Etta held in a sob as the floor creaked beneath her. The guard didn't turn.

"I know you're there," he said. "And I know you possess an even greater magic than her." He glanced sideways and nudged the body with his toe.

Power tingled in Etta's fingertips. If they were outside, she'd have him flat on the ground already. But there was no living earth to manipulate inside.

A horse neighed outside and fear sparked through her. More guards? She knew she should run, but her eyes stared into her mother's empty gaze and she couldn't move.

The guard finally turned to her. He opened his mouth to speak again but shut it as his eyes widened.

"Leave her alone," a high-pitched, but strong voice commanded behind her.

Tears dripped down Etta's cheeks as she turned to the newcomer and ran to him. He caught her in a hug.

"Are you okay?" Alex, the Crown Prince of Gaule, asked her softly.

She sobbed against his chest.

Alex was a few years older than her, but they'd been friends since she was born.

Another figure appeared behind Alex and lunged at the guard. He'd been too stunned by the prince's presence that he hadn't been ready for an attack.

Etta watched without emotion as her father ran his sword through the man's neck. The guard dropped and her father didn't bother to clean the dripping blade before shoving it into its sheath and marching toward her.

"I came to warn you," Alex said. "My father is coming for magic folk."

Her father's face was frigid as he ripped her like a ragdoll from the prince's grip. "We don't need a warning from you," he spat, looking back at his dead wife. "I save the kingdom and your father betrays me." He pointed one long finger. "There will come a day, Alexandre Durand, when my family will be the death of yours."

The threat sat heavy in the air as Etta's father lifted her into the wagon. She wept as she looked back at the place where they were forced to leave her mother. As she met the prince's gaze, he too had tears in his eyes.

Etta woke gasping for air. She wiped at her damp face and sat up. Darkness enveloped the woods around her. It was the time most people locked themselves inside, away from roaming spirits. For her, she reveled in the silence of the stars that could be seen through gaps in the trees, glittering like rare gems. She liked to believe her mother was among them.

They hadn't traveled far from the castle the night of her death. Her family's curse tied her father to the king, as it would soon tie her to Alex, meaning they had to stay close, lest the invisible tie tighten around her father's neck like a noose.

Alex was the boy born into the wrong family. He'd been too good for them, but he'd been a child. Now, with older eyes, she saw him as no different from the rest of his cruel family.

The night of their escape, her father told her everything about the curse.

La Dame set out to ruin Bela and its rulers in the cruelest possible way.

She knew her future led to Prince Alexandre. She would protect him. She would fight for him. But he was the prince of the kingdom that killed her mother and continued to hunt her people, so her trust, her friendship, was something he would never have again.

CHAPTER 3

The taut string of the bow quivered against Etta's fingers as she lined up her shot and tracked her target. She pulled her arm back, feeling the soft feathers of the arrow against her skin. Loosing the arrow, she cursed when it flew wide of the fox. The animal ran off, probably to harass someone else. She'd been tracking it for hours, because it had been causing havoc for a few of the families nearby.

She threw the bow down in frustration. It was a skill she'd never been able to master. A stick snapped to her right, and she caught sight of a deer, its head bent, lost in its own hunger.

Etta slid a knife from her belt and flipped it once in her hand. With the stealth of a thief, she stalked toward it unseen. Only the soft crunch beneath her feet told of her presence.

The deer snapped its head up, but before it could run, Etta flicked her wrist and sent the knife flying end over end. It struck the deer in the chest. The deer ran and Etta chased it for a few paces before gripping the second knife and throwing it as hard as the first.

There was no satisfaction as there would have been with the fox. The deer did not mean any harm, but resources were scarce and this meat might fetch a price at market. Etta knelt beside the dying creature and told the grasses to rise up to create a softer bed for it to die on. She stroked it between the eyes and a quiver ran through him before his chest failed to rise.

He wasn't a sizable deer so Etta was able to heft it up across her shoulders, grunting from the effort. She trudged the short distance to her cabin and by the time she arrived, her shoulders screamed from the strain. She dropped the deer on the ground outside the door and shook out her arms. The deer's eyes bore into her but there was no life behind them.

Her father hadn't returned. Sometimes he would leave for many days at a time, needing to be close to the castle to soothe the strain of the curse. He tried to hide it, but even the short distance from the king pained him. Would she feel the same crushing agony every time she left Alexandre's side?

She pulled at the collar of her shirt as her breaths thickened. She had to get out of the forest if for no other reason than for the distraction. Her destiny rushed towards her faster than she could stop it and she wasn't ready.

Her eyes flicked back to the deer. She hasn't expected to find one and as much as she wanted to climb on Verite and ride away, she couldn't leave the meat to spoil.

She raised her hand to brush her hair back and paused, the corners of her mouth tipping up and a plan forming. The meat would fetch a fair price at market if she made the journey to the village.

It had been too long since she left the forest. She'd barely spoken to anyone other than her father or Vérité. Her father would be furious until she dropped the money from her sale into his hands.

Wanting to get moving, she clutched her knife. Without her father's help, she couldn't hang the deer, and she was too anxious to get on the road to let it age. No, she'd have to do this the bloodier way.

She didn't enjoy butchering, but she preferred to get it done quickly. Some things were just necessary for survival. Her father taught her that blood was nothing to be scared of. One day, she'd be asked to spill a lot of it.

It was well into the afternoon when she finished and wrapped the meat in paper. The market would be closing in a few hours. She'd never make it in time so she'd need to leave in the morning.

As she got to her feet and shook out her stiff legs, she looked down at her shirt and trousers, both covered with blood. With a sigh, she headed off toward the river.

Etta woke early and donned a simple dress that would make her blend in rather than stand out. It was a commoner's dress. The merchants would think her a farmer or merely a hunter's wife. No one would ever guess the true line she was descended from, the kingdom crushed by a curse.

Outside, Etta whistled a single high note and waited. Vérité appeared in no time. He never roamed far. "I'm sorry, my friend," she said. "We cannot stand out. As I must wear this ridiculous dress today, you must dress the part as well."

She took a saddle from its hook on the wall. Vérité snorted but offered no further resistance. He was smarter than most people she'd known.

Placing her wares for the market in the saddle bags, Etta climbed on and squeezed her legs against the horse's sides. They communicated through subtle shifts and slight kicks, but for the most part, the horse understood what she wanted. Theirs was a special bond. He was a wild horse, untamed. She'd had the wildness trained out of her. She was lethal, but Vérité was understanding. Together, they were complete.

They rode for hours before leaving the safety of the woods behind and cantered down the path toward town.

Rows and rows of stone and wood structures stretched out before her. The dirt path gave way to smooth brick roads. Shops were plentiful. While magic folk were hidden away in the forest, the people of Gaule thrived. She shook her head and urged Vérité forward. Disgust twisted in her belly for these people. Every time she ventured among them, it was the same. Their ancestors had destroyed her family's kingdom generations ago and now they'd destroyed her people.

Pushing it away, she pasted a pleasant look on her face, not the look of a thief or trained fighter. Just a girl enjoying a ride on her horse. She came to a stop in the middle of the market square. Merchants busied themselves setting up booths for the day. She could take it directly to the butcher shop, but he'd most likely try to underpay her. His people working the booth were easier to manipulate.

A woman lifted her gaze up from where she set out a display of dried and salted meat as Etta slid down from Vérité's back. She was the butcher's wife, but no more pleasant than him.

They were too near the cobbler she'd been caught stealing from last time she came to town for her comfort. Her shoes were once again worn to the point of discomfort, but they were better than the ones she'd had that day.

Poverty didn't bother her. She wasn't on this earth to live in comfort. Her training and hard circumstances were meant to prepare her. She was only born to fulfill the curse.

Silently, Etta unhooked the bag from Vérité's saddle and walked forward.

The butcher's wife eyed her suspiciously and opened the bag.

"Steal this, hmmm?" Her voice cracked as she wheezed.

"What?" Etta leaned forward to begin taking the packed meat out. Her braid fell over one shoulder. "I made the kill with my own hands."

"You always say that, Darlin', but that don't make it so." She picked up a pack and sniffed at it. "This don't smell so fresh."

"That's bullshit. I butchered it yesterday."

"Probably did a hack job on it."

Etta gripped the edge of the booth in fury.

The butcher's wife continued. "Where you find it? We don't get much venison around here. Sometimes the hunters find deer in that meadow east of town."

She was testing her. The meadow east of town held nothing more than a patch of grass. No hunter would bother with it.

Etta narrowed her eyes. "The Black Forest."

The older woman's eyes widened. "Don't you lie to me, girl."

"I have never lied to you." She leaned toward her. "Some of us don't fear the spirits." She didn't mention that the spirits were just people, her people, cloaked by her father's wards.

"Simpleminded girl."

Etta shook her head. "How much for the meat?"

The woman put a handful of coins down on the table—half its worth.

Etta growled. "You must think I really am a simpleminded girl. I won't sell it for that." She reached for the packs of meat to put them back into her bag.

The butcher's wife stopped her with an iron grip on her wrist. "Guards," she yelled, looking around for the guards that were a constant presence in town. "Thief!" She gave Etta a wicked smile before false panic crossed her face.

Etta yanked her arm free and scooped up the coins from the table. Vérité neighed nearby, and she whipped her head around to watch a guard grab his reins, preventing her from escaping on horseback.

Cursing the dress she wore, she lifted her skirt and took off. Reclaiming Vérité would be a problem for later, once she got out of this mess. The guards would believe the word of that wretched woman over a girl with no connection to the town. As she ran through the streets, two guards crashed along behind her, shoving stunned people out of the way.

A sense of deja vu hit her as she turned into a narrow alleyway between two shops. She knew the underside of this town almost as well as she knew her forest. Her chest heaved, but her legs could keep going all day. Glancing quickly behind her, she knew that wasn't the case for her pursuers. Her lips curved up at the thought. Easy.

Feeling for the knife hidden in a sheath down the front of her dress, she picked up speed. The alley narrowed further and ended with a stone barrier that blocked it from the next street.

Pumping her arms, she did a running jump, landing on top of it. Her feet only touched briefly before she sailed toward the other side where another guard waited for her. She bowled him over as she flew through the air and they both crashed to the ground. Her shoulder screamed in protest when she deftly rolled to her feet and freed her knife.

The guard was slower getting up, but drew his sword as he did. A knife could never match a sword and as the steel flashed before her, all she could do was duck.

"Madam, you are under arrest." He grunted as he tried to force her against the wall to end the fight. She whirled to the side, but his sword stopped her, slicing across her arm in the process.

She bit her lip to keep from screaming and spotted a place where weeds broke through the brick on the ground. Without thinking, she willed the weeds to keep growing. The guard looked at her curiously, still pinning her against the wall, as she narrowed her eyes in concentration.

"What?" His eyes widened at the growing weeds tangling around his ankles. "Magic."

She paid him no mind as her power overwhelmed her, buzzing through her like a brilliant high. The weeds traveled up his legs, and he released her to slash at them with his sword. They didn't stop until they were tied about his shoulders, holding him in place. For good measure, she flicked her finger, causing a weed to grow over his mouth just as he began to scream.

Her father's voice entered her mind. He'd be furious, but adrenaline rushed in her veins.

"Someone is sure to find you." She shrugged and slid her knife back down the front of her dress as she turned to walk away.

A teenage girl stood at the far entrance to the alley, her eyes like round saucers.

Fear surged through Etta. Two people had seen her magic today. They would come after her. It was the law. Only then did she realize her idiocy.

She raced toward the girl and as she neared, she realized the girl was older than she first appeared. Probably only a few years younger than Etta herself.

Etta opened her mouth to speak, to plead with the girl for secrecy, but the girl held up a hand.

"Come with me," she said.

"I'm not going anywhere with you."

"I know who you are, Etta. And unless you want them to catch you, come."

Etta had no choice but to follow her to the healer's shop.

"I know what you think you saw out there," Etta began. "But it wasn't what it seemed."

"Things are never as they seem." She smiled kindly, pushing her black curls away from her shoulders. Her golden-brown face was round and soft, holding none of the sharp angles hard living had created in Etta.

"My name is Maiya," she said.

Etta snapped her gaze to the other girl. "How do you know my name?"

Maiya laughed and it had an airy quality to it. "Everyone in town knows you. You're the girl who shows up on occasion and causes a ruckus. No one knows where you come from or who your people are. You're a mystery." She paused. "You're also Viktor's daughter. I saw you enter the village."

Etta grunted.

"Your arm is injured." Maiya gestured at the blood trickling from a shallow cut. "Have a seat, I can fix it." She led Etta to a stool that sat in front of a table littered with various healing tools and potions. Grateful for the first bit of kindness she'd experienced from anyone in town, Etta accepted the help and held out her arm. She expected Maiya to pick up one of her needles or ointments. Instead, the girl ran her palm down Etta's arm and closed her eyes.

Etta's skin began to shift and pull together. Heat seared into her arm. She yanked it away in shock and a twinge of pain, but Maiya was done. Where there had been a red, seeping slice a moment before, it was now only pink skin, a bit paler than the weathered skin surrounding it.

"You ..." Etta stuttered. "You have healing magic."

Maiya smiled. "We all have secrets, my friend. Now you hold my life in your hands as much as I hold yours."

Before she could respond, two loud voices sounded outside the front door seconds before two men pushed it open. She recognized her father immediately and slid from the stool.

"She must do it," her father was saying.

"Do you think this is really the way? The risk is—"

"Acceptable. If she doesn't fulfill this curse, the pain will be too great. I live with this distance between myself and the king—my charge—every day and I wouldn't wish it on her."

"Father." Etta stepped forward and the two men noticed their daughters for the first time. "What risk is too great? I can handle anything."

Her father smiled proudly for a brief moment before he charged forward angrily. "What are you doing here, Persinette? You know you aren't allowed to leave the forest."

"But I killed a deer. We've been running so desperately low on supplies, I decided to sell it." She held out her hand to reveal the coins.

He cursed under his breath. "When the guards started charging into the market, I saw you. If I hadn't sent Maiya to find you, what was your plan?"

When she didn't respond, he continued. "They found a guard near here tangled in weeds. Know anything about that?"

She shook her head. "No father."

"Well, apparently he doesn't either. We just passed by someone questioning him and he claims no magic was involved, but dammit! He was tied in weeds. Who is going to believe that? I don't even have time to contemplate why that guard is lying when I have to worry about what happens if he suddenly becomes truthful. I taught you better."

She hung her head. "Yes, Father."

He took the coins from her. "How did you get here?"

"Vérité."

He cursed again. "I told you to stay away from that horse. He can't be tamed."

"Well, they took him. I need to get him back."

"Not happening. Confiscated horses belong to the crown. He's probably already on his way to the castle stables."

She couldn't believe she'd let him down. Vérité was her best friend. He deserved to be free, roaming the woods at will, not cooped up in a stall.

"Remove it from your mind." Her father looked to the other man and then back at her. "This is Pierre. I see you've met Maiya. Read this." He shoved a folded paper at her.

She carefully opened it. Scrawled in black ink were instructions for a tournament.

One week.
A battle of the kingdom's greatest warriors.
To the death.
The winner will become the prince's champion.

She closed her eyes, breathing deeply to calm her erratic heart. *To the death.* Who would give their life willingly to stand at the prince's side? Fools. All of them.

She jerked her head up, reading the sign again. She wasn't a fool, but she was cursed.

The day after her mother's death- the first day of their lives in hiding, Etta's father had begun training her. Sometimes it was all the two of them had. The past was gone. The future was dark. They'd lived each day to become the best they could. It was perfect. Her way in.

"How is it that just as I need a way into the palace, this opportunity arises?"

Her father studied her for a moment. "Tradition."

"Yes, but what does that mean, father?"

He rubbed his chin. "Every king, or king-to-be in Alexandre's case, has a protector. Someone to stand at their side and fight for them. The royals of Gaule don't even know the origins of their own traditions. This one arose when the first to bend to the curse abandoned Bela to swear allegiance to Gaule. Since that time, no king has forgone their oath-man. Basile's have been finding ways to hold the position, not all under the Basile name. Now it is your turn."

"I can do it," she vowed, raising her eyes to look at her father. "In one week, I will begin my fulfillment of the curse, but Father, I am the last. It ends with me. This is my promise. I will break it. Only death can stop me. And then I'll bring them down. The family Durand has controlled the Basiles for far too long."

"Greater than you have tried and failed."

His words hammered into her, his lack of faith sending a spark of pain through her heart. Etta squared her shoulders and held her head high. "This ends with me."

CHAPTER 4

The palace teemed with activity in preparation for the tournament.

Alex sat atop the outer wall, looking across the grounds surrounding it. Guards marched up the road from the wide-open iron gates. It was rare that they closed them. There were no threats to the kingdom while the wards held around their borders.

The wards. It struck him as ironic that the kingdom's only protection was the very magic they'd done their best to eliminate. The man who created the wards spent years in service to the crown before his magic made him a threat.

That wasn't what clouded the prince's thoughts today, though. Many men were going to die. All to have an honored place at his side. He kept telling himself they entered willingly. None of it would be his fault. He would observe the tournament as if it was the great entertainment it was supposed to be.

Tents stretched across the horizon, their pointed roofs reaching toward the brilliant sun. People traveled from all across the kingdom for the spectacle. Entertainers had livened up the evening for the past few days and flooded the markets in the afternoons. Knights and other warriors arrived in droves.

"Thought I'd find you here," Tyson said, taking a seat and dropping his legs over the edge of the wall. "Today is going to be epic."

Alex shot him a forced smile and looked away. His brother saw such events with a child's excitement. He didn't remember a time when Gaule was sending its soldiers out to die across the border.

Alex didn't know why he needed a protector when they were at peace. But the people needed the tournament. As awful as it was, it brought them together, and they expected it.

"Have you checked out those tunnels I told you about?" Tyson asked.

"I haven't exactly had time, little brother." Alex glanced sideways at him.

"Don't tell Father about them until you do, because you have to see them before he destroys them."

"That's what should be done, anyway."

"Why? With the wards in place, it's not like magic folk can use them."

Alex couldn't fault his brother's logic, so he let it go and got to his feet. "I need to prepare."

Tyson snorted. "I know you, Alex. You're about to go down into that madness and you're going to ditch your guards to do it." He gestured toward the crowds. They crowded around the arena that had been built specifically for the event. "Can I come?"

Alex laughed. "Father is going to be pissed."

Tyson shrugged, a mischievous shine in his eyes.

Alex laughed again. "Let's go."

The two princes changed out of their padded silken surcoats, replacing them with shortened tunics made of plain woven fabric. They removed every bit of gold jewelry and discarded the solid gold circlets their father insisted they wear atop their heads. Alex donned his chain mail despite the heat. He'd look like just another man arriving for the fight. His jeweled sword would be too obvious, so he strapped a sheathed knife to his waist instead, not like he would use it. Tyson hadn't been wrong. Alex's fighting skills left a lot to be desired. He tried, he did. He just lacked the interest his brother had. The last thing Alex did was pull his chain mail coif over his head. He grimaced as the weight settled around him, but it would help him go unnoticed.

"Your Highnesses," someone called as they stepped back into the courtyard.

Alex groaned and turned toward Geoff who was hurrying toward them. He served in the prince's guard and thought that meant he had full control of Alex. He hadn't tried to hide his disdain for this competition. He thought he should be named protector. The king obviously hadn't agreed. And Geoff hadn't entered into the competition. He wasn't brave enough.

"I'm afraid I must ask where you think you're going?" he asked.

"Relax, Geoff." Tyson sidled up beside him and flung an arm across his shoulders. The guard stiffened. "I think you just need some rest."

Confusion clouded Geoff's face, and he tried to shrug off the adolescent prince.

Before he could respond, Tyson's free arm flew through the air and connected with the side of his head with a loud crunch. The guard collapsed against the wall and slid down, unconscious.

"Told you sleep would help." Tyson shook out his fist. "That guy's head is hard."

Alex stared at his brother as he tried to contain his laughter. "What..."

Tyson grinned. "Always wanted to hit that guy."

"You do know Father is going to punish you for doing something that won't even help us get out of here?"

"What's he going to do? Lock me in my room again?"

"It was a week, and he barely sent any food up." Alex shook his head in disbelief.

"Good thing my maid is in love with me."

Alex barked out a laugh. "She's got many years on you."

"Doesn't make a difference when you're this adorable." He looked around. "Come on."

Tyson caused all sorts of trouble in the palace and he was a thorn in their father's side, but at times like these, it was good having him around.

Alex followed him to an empty chamber at the back of the palace chapel. A door led them to a tunnel through the outer wall.

"I don't want to know how you know this is here," Alex started. "Or how you have a key to that door."

"You'd be amazed at the secrets this place holds. Before the wards, Father had many spies. He met them in the chapel, using the tunnel to smuggle them in and out."

The wall wasn't terribly thick, so they were outside in no time.

Tyson started running down the hill toward the rows of tents. "Come on. I want to see the fighters before the festivities begin."

The crowd engulfed them. Two large soldiers passed Alex, jostling him. He spun to keep from falling and lost sight of his brother. People beckoned to him as he walked, selling everything from jewelry to swords to various foods. Spices wafted through the air, assaulting him from all directions.

A knight rode by atop a mountainous horse, larger than many in the palace stables. His armor crashed together as he moved.

Even with his headpiece obscuring his dusky hair and forehead, Alex avoided looking directly at anyone lest they recognize him as he went in search of Tyson. He walked toward the clusters of fighting men, knowing that was where he'd find his brother.

Tyson appeared up ahead, weaving in and out of people, so he picked up his pace. Alex opened his mouth to call to him and came to a jolting stop as he collided with someone.

He barely moved but the other person went sprawling onto the stones. His eyes caught the long golden hair and traveled down to the girl's face. She looked up at him and the softness faded away as her green eyes flashed.

Her strange beauty stuck him momentarily. "I'm terribly sorry, my lady." He extended a hand to help her and smiled kindly. "I was not watching my steps."

"I can tell." Ignoring his offered hand, she jumped to her feet with a surprising agility and brushed her hands down her plain dress.

A peasant. The prince made the distinction immediately. The hard lines of her face suggested she was accustomed to tough work. A farmer's daughter, perhaps. Maybe even a farmer's wife, although she was awfully young.

She looked behind her as if she would run and a stroke of familiarity struck Alex.

"Have we met before?" he asked.

Her eyes narrowed. "I wouldn't have cause to visit the palace."

He grinned. She recognized him. That was a start. "Your Highness."

"What?"

"You obviously know who I am, so it's customary to show your respect."

She laughed, finally cracking a smile. It wasn't kind exactly, but it was there. "I'll show my respect when you've earned it."

"What's that supposed to mean?"

She crossed her arms over her chest. "All you've done is run me over."

"I am your prince."

She mumbled something under her breath that sounded a lot like "Not my prince" and it made him smile wider. He couldn't remember the last time someone was so blatantly rude to him. He found it quite amusing.

“Why are you smiling like that?” She scowled.

“Like what?” His eyes widened innocently.

She pointed to his face. “Like I’m a child who just spoke for the very first time.”

He laughed. “I like you.”

“I don’t like you,” she countered.

“Believe it or not, that is what I find so enchanting.”

“I am not enchanting.” She pressed her lips into a flat line.

“No.” He narrowed his eyes. “You’re... fierce.” His eyes lit up. “That’s it. Well, fierce lady...” He bowed, sweeping one arm out to the side. “May I have the pleasure of your name?”

“No.”

He should have walked away. He needed to forget about this overly bold girl. But his feet wouldn't move. An invisible pull kept him there. Their eyes connected, hers pleading with him to go.

"Alex." Tyson's voice cut through the tension as he stepped between them. "Are you going to introduce me to your friend?" He smiled easily.

"I am not his friend." The girl turned and walked toward the rows of tents.

Alex watched her until she disappeared.

Tyson clapped a hand on his shoulder. "I don't think she liked you, Brother. Did you tell her you were a prince?"

"That made it worse."

Tyson laughed. "I like her already."

Alex shook his head, not sure what happened. He didn't even know her name. She was only a peasant. But more than anything, he yearned to speak to her again.

CHAPTER 5

Shaken by her run-in with the prince, Etta sat in her tent with her head in her hands. Alex hadn't recognized her. If he had, she'd be in chains by now.

As soon as she'd seen him, she'd wanted to run, to get away from this entire curse. Her feet hadn't let her. Her entire body hummed at the closeness.

As soon as the thought filled the space in her mind, she conjured up an image of the boy she'd known all those years ago, finding it hard to believe that he would ever hurt her.

But she knew what his family did to hers. Eight years was a long time. He'd been by his father's side as they hunted the magic folk throughout the kingdom.

The entire plan relied on him not knowing Etta was the same person as the Persinette he'd befriended. She'd never be allowed a position in the palace if they knew she had magic. She didn't know what they'd do to her.

Maiya pushed through the tent flap with her father in tow. Etta's own father wasn't there. She'd shed no tears when they said their goodbyes in the early hours of the morning. If she managed to survive the tournament, she'd move into the palace to serve at the prince's side and seeing her father would be a near impossibility.

Viktor Basile was the most notorious outlaw in Gaule. He risked everything every time he went to town. There was no way he could show his face amid the crowds here for the tournament.

Etta looked up at Maiya, the girl she'd befriended only a week ago. There were tears in her eyes. "Are you sure you have to do this?"

Etta glanced at Pierre and he nodded, letting her know his daughter could handle the truth.

"I am a descendant of Bela, just as you are, but I am also more than that." She stood, straightened her shoulders. "I am from the royal line."

Maiya's eyes widened. "You're the cursed." Her gasp reverberated around the space.

Anger ripped through her heart. Not at the girl in front of her. Not even at her father. The anger was for her ancestors. King Phillip and Queen Aurora destroyed the kingdom of Bela and doomed their future generations to forever be under the control of La Dame.

Her father would tell her to push that anger away. Emotion only hindered in a fight. But she was not her father. She would use it to win this championship and to bring this kingdom to its knees.

"Do not cry for me, Maiya." Etta softened her eyes. "Many before me have taken up the curse." She looked at each of them. "I will be no different. If I have to fight my way to that heinous prince's side then I will do it. I can do it. If things were different, I would be a princess of Bela. It is my duty to represent our people well."

The alternative was too sad. She's watched her father go through the separation from the man he'd been cursed to protect. It wasn't the kind of life anyone wanted. Even a future inside the palace of Gaule, a future of hiding her magic, was better than that.

Pierre's eyes glossed over, and pride shone through. It was not the grudging pride her father showed when she mastered a new part of her training. It was something else. He lowered himself to one knee and Etta froze.

Maiya followed her father's lead.

"Bela is no more," he rasped. "But I see it in you." He placed a hand over his heart. "Princess."

Etta stumbled back, fighting tears. These were her people, people of Bela, the kingdom she'd never known but always carried in her heart.

They weren't the first Belaens she'd met. The forest served as home to many of them. But they were the first who knew her for a Basile, a descendant of the last kings. And they loved her for it. Their kingdom was gone because of the curse of her family, yet here they knelt.

Despair crashed into her and she couldn't breathe. Clutching at her chest, she gasped until her lungs expanded. It was too much. All of it. Reality was suffocating. Any minute, she would walk out among those people and fight for her life. She couldn't use her magic.

Maiya stood and rushed forward to wrap her arms around Etta.

Pierre was slower getting to his feet. "Persinette Basile, the strength of Bela runs through your veins. You only have to find it. You must prepare. I'll wait outside."

"We believe in you," Maiya whispered, releasing her.

Belief. It was like an infusion of power. This was happening. By the end of the tournament, she'd either be the victor or nothing at all.

She refused to be nothing.

Drying her face, Etta nodded to Maiya, unable to voice her gratitude.

Maiya didn't speak as she helped Etta dress to be better suited for the fight to come. She donned a lightweight mail shirt that wouldn't help much against heavy blows, but also wouldn't hinder her speed. She bound her hair up tight against her head and slid the helmet into place. Her sword hung heavy at her waist. They were allowed two weapons. She preferred the simplicity of staffs, but it wouldn't be enough. Many of the others would choose spears, but her greatest skills resided with the knives.

Running her fingers over the curved blade, she caught her reflection in the shining steel. Glacial eyes stared back at her.

Cold was better than dead.

"Come on." She sheathed her knife and pushed the tent flap aside.

Maiya walked on her right and Pierre joined them on her left.

Laughter erupted around them as they pushed through the crowd.

"Look who's trying to play soldier," someone yelled.

Another was bolder. "Girl, you don't need to die to get our attention. I'd be happy to give you some back at my tent."

Etta scowled but otherwise ignored them. She had no intention of dying. The walk to the newly built arena stretched out before her as the catcalls faded from her mind. All she could see was the wooden rail and the place behind it. An open space was surrounded by barriers and platforms. Wooden structures spotted the arena, built to make the fights more entertaining.

Etta's bottom lip curved up. It was perfect. She could do this.

Placing her hands on the smooth wood of the rail, Etta leaped over it and turned back to Maiya and Pierre. Opening her mouth to say something, the words failed her, and she closed it again.

Pierre gave her a fierce stare before ushering his daughter away. They would be watching. Along with everyone in the kingdom.

The men standing in the center of the arena glared at her and she faltered when she saw them. A few laughed, others ignored her entirely.

A horn sounded and the people lining the rails began to cheer. The fighters turned toward the raised platform as the king stepped up, followed by the queen and their three children.

The king kept all emotion from his face as he scanned the ranks of warriors, most of whom would be dead by tournament's end. The queen couldn't look at them at all.

Alex seemed conflicted, almost scared. As a boy, he'd never cared for blood.

Princess Camille looked very much like her father. She was more suited to follow in his footsteps than her older brother.

Tyson had a child's excitement in his eyes. But then, he'd probably never seen anyone die.

Etta watched them, searching for something, anything, to fuel her hatred. They gave it to her. It was easy for them.

None of this was supposed to be easy.

Hiding at the back of the group, she waited.

"Today is a great day." The king's voice boomed. "A protector is an oath-man. It's a sacred partnership between king and warrior."

Etta clenched her teeth. It was so sacred that the king tried to kill his own oath-man for his magic.

The king continued. "To all of the men here to fight today, you are the best our kingdom has. Each and every one of you has an unmatched honor." He motioned to Prince Alexandre.

Alex stepped forward, clearing his throat nervously. Then his nervousness disappeared and a cool mask settled over his features.

"Good luck." He flicked his hand toward the warriors, barely even sparing a glance. "Let the first battle commence."

Thankful she wasn't first, Etta followed the others out of the arena to wait. A large man in full armor passed, and a shiver ran through her. She clutched the hilt of her sword at her waist.

The first battle ended in minutes and two guards dragged the body away. The second went much the same way. In the third, both men ended up killing each other.

When Etta's name was called, she barely heard it over the pounding in her ears. The drums began as they had for each pairing before her. The beat vibrated in her chest, matching the heavy rhythm of her heart. The blood-thirsty crowd yelled and chanted as she stepped forward. Lost in her own mind as she walked by a trail of blood, she barely heard the laughter and jeers thrown her way.

Her opponent dwarfed her and wore a guard's uniform. He'd been trained at the palace. The thought comforted her. Her earliest training had been there as well. In the years since, she'd studied the guards, knew their patterns for one day she knew she'd be among them.

Normal armor had weaknesses—the neck, the joints. The king tried to fix those, having armor made for his guards that protected their most vulnerable spots.

It was brilliant craftsmanship, but it sacrificed free movement and speed. Etta might have been thought foolish for her light armor, but she'd exit the arena with her life because of it.

The guard faced her. The drums stopped. The crowd leaned forward.

He bowed to her, and she hated that she had to kill him, even if he was a guard.

She inclined her head and drew her sword. He attacked, shifting his weight onto his front foot to jab his sword forward.

She knocked it aside and cursed herself for being on the defense right at the start. He lunged and their swords crashed together, his strength against her will. She spun to the side and ducked another blow with a low roll. Popping back up to her feet, she ran, ignoring the laughter of the spectators as she ducked behind a barrier.

His footsteps thudded against the ground as he searched her out. Sheathing her sword, she pulled her knife and tucked it between her teeth as she reached up with both arms to grip the top of the barrier and pull herself up.

Crouching low, knife in hand, she waited for him to get near before flinging herself off and slamming into him. He roared as her knife bounced off his armor and he flung her off. She took his helmet with her, revealing a scarred face, the face of a man who'd been in many battles before.

He ran to where he'd laid his spear and dropped his sword to retrieve it. Etta grinned, knowing she must look crazed. The guards loved their spears and Etta loved that they were easier to beat than a sword.

He ran toward her and lunged. She ducked away from the spear and spun to deliver a hard kick to his back. He stumbled forward but didn't fall.

"I'm going to gut you, girl," the guard yelled, moving slowly.

If there hadn't been eyes on them, she could've bested him in an instant with her magic.

He backed her up against the barrier and she looked for a way out. His knee came up and knocked the knife from her fingers. He brought his spear forward and she dropped low. The spearhead embedded itself in the wood, stunning him for a moment. Before he could yank it free, she sprang back up and jumped to kick both her feet at his chest. He fell back and she pulled his spear free, not hesitating before spinning it around like she'd done with her pole against her father so many times before.

Her father's voice entered her mind. *When it's time to take the killing blow, hesitancy will end you. There is no mercy in war.*

The guard's hands reached for the spear, but she knocked them away seconds before plunging the tip into his neck. Blood spurted past the steel head and she gave one final shove before letting go and stepping back.

The crowd stayed silent for a long moment before they roared in approval. Approval of her, of what she did. Her hands shook, so she clasped them together and turned to the royal family. Their eyes were wide. Her armor didn't hide the fact that she was a woman, but her size hid her skill.

The king rose once the crowd quieted to hear him speak. "Congratulations. Please, remove your helmet and give us the honor of your name."

She obeyed. Her sweat-soaked hair clung to her head as she pulled the helmet off.

"I am Etta."

"Do you have a last name, Etta?"

"No."

The king accepted that, but the prince sprang from his throne and his eyes burned into her.

Her curse tugged at her, wanting to be near him.

She sucked in a breath and shifted her eyes away.

If she won, would he accept a woman as his protector?

They were going to find out.

CHAPTER 6

Etta heard no remarks as she walked back to her tent. Exhaustion weighed her down, making every step harder than the one before it. The crowd parted for her, a stunned wariness among them. Etta wasn't supposed to survive the first round. Certainly not against one of the crown's own guards.

Maiya and Pierre followed at a distance, for which Etta was grateful. She did not have any words for them. She craved the solitude of her woods, the calm company of Vérité. Her magic pulsed in her fingertips, wanting an escape. Fingertips that were now stained red.

When Etta pushed into her tent, she could still hear the commotion from the arena. A new fight started. Her breath wheezed in her chest and she clutched at her armor as the adrenaline left her body and reality came crashing in. She was alive. The first of four fights were over and there she was, standing tall.

Only, she didn't feel like she'd won anything.

Tears stung her eyes as she tried to lift the chain mail off her shoulders. Maiya and Pierre entered quietly.

"I can't get it off," Etta yelled. "Get it off me!"

Maiya moved toward her silently and gripped the bottom of the mail shirt, sliding it up. Blood ran between the links. Etta's clothing underneath had sweat sticking it to her skin.

"Father," Maiya said softly, signaling him with her eyes.

He lowered his head and left the way he'd come.

Etta dropped to her knees in front of a basin of water and plunged her hands in. Blood swirled on the surface as she scrubbed. A sob escaped her throat and she didn't stop until her skin was raw.

It wasn't deer's blood this time.

How was she supposed to fulfill the curse when she'd be asked to do this time and again? Years ago, when she was barely more than a child, she'd thought it would be better to be dead than to kill for her enemies. She wouldn't have been the first curse bearer in her line to consider it.

But she was not them. The day her father told her of the curse was the day she'd decided she'd be the one to break it. First, she needed to obey it.

Maiya laid her hands on the back of Etta's neck and calmness flowed into her as she bowed her head, trying to steady her breathing. The girl's healing magic acted as a tonic to her tarnished soul.

Etta let her power flow in harmony with Maiya's, a bright green bud sprouting through the dull and lifeless ground. Her heart calmed and she closed her eyes. When she opened them again, she'd regained control of her own emotions.

Etta finished cleaning herself as best she could with the small basin and changed into a simple dress. After her fight, she doubted anyone would underestimate her anymore, but it wouldn't hurt for them to see her as just a girl.

Maiya finished putting flowers in Etta's hair as Pierre returned.

"Come with me." He led them from the tent, but not back toward the crowds. Instead, they went further into town, not stopping until they reached the healer's shop.

"Father," Etta gasped, running to him as soon as the door slammed shut.

He gathered her into his arms, squeezing her tightly in relief. They'd never been very affectionate, but for the first time since before her fight, Etta felt safe.

"I couldn't stay away," he said.

"But what if someone recognizes you?"

"I know how to keep out of sight." He released her. "I saw you fight today."

"I didn't hesitate."

"No, my daughter. I am so very proud of you."

He'd never uttered those words before and the strength she'd felt before the fight began to return. "I wish I could return to the forest."

His face fell. "This curse takes everything we love." He cupped her cheek. "Don't hold on to the forest. Don't wish after me. It will only lead to despair."

"Maybe I can beat it."

"No, Persinette. It cannot be overcome, only endured."

"But you don't have to fulfill it. You're cursed and you live in the forest, away from the palace."

He closed his eyes briefly. "And I feel like I'm dying. If I could be at the king's side, I would. Every day apart takes something more from me. I am in pain, Etta, and so very tired. I want more for you than a life of misery."

"We should be returning lest anyone miss us." Pierre stepped forward.

Her father nodded. "I am afraid our lives are very much without hope, but don't let them beat you. Keep vigilant. Never trust a Durand and try to find some happiness anywhere you can."

"Why do you sound like you're saying goodbye forever?" Tears welled in her eyes.

"Because your path is only beginning. It isn't safe for us to speak again, but during the fights to come, know that I am watching. I am here."

She shook her head. "I'm going to find a way, Father. I'm going to free us both."

"Don't spend your life working for something that can't be done." He stepped away from her and she felt Pierre's firm grip on her arm.

She stopped at the threshold of the door. "Believe in me, Father."

No words followed her as she stepped into the street and made her way back to the place where it was all beginning. She dried her face and vowed that she would see her father again.

If the first fight had been a raging battle, the second was a pure slaughter. The compact man she'd been paired with had no hope. She disarmed him only minutes into the fight and held out her sword as he lunged for her with his fists. He impaled himself on the blade without even a thrust from her.

His eyes met hers in surprised anguish and she held his gaze, giving him that bit of respect.

He didn't deserve to die.

None of them did.

When she faced the king for the second time, her face transformed into a cool mask of indifference. She dropped her sword to the ground as the crowd began to cheer at her back. She hated them for it.

The king didn't speak this time and the queen's face held a sickly pallor. Prince Alexandre leaned back in his seat wearily as if this tournament was taking a toll on him personally. Etta narrowed her eyes. He'd never had to look death in the face and end up delivering the killing blow.

"Well done, Etta." Princess Camille spoke after a few moments of silence. She clutched her cane as she stood, her mangled foot dragging as she stepped forward.

Etta didn't respond, knowing a thank you was expected for the compliment. She refused to be grateful for anything. The killing skill was not something to be proud of.

Camille waited for an acknowledgment. Etta's gut churned. She'd heard the stories of the cruel princess who wanted nothing more than vengeance on the magic folk for her disability. One the night the purge began, a guard with magic took it upon himself to direct his power at the princess's horse in the moments before his death. The horse threw her to the ground and trampled her leg as he pranced wildly with the magical energy.

Dark eyes narrowed, but she gave a jerk of her head, dismissing Etta.

Etta breathed out and scanned the crowd, looking for any sign of her father, knowing there would be none. He was a ghost. Undetectable.

The killing move was not a shock as it had been after her first fight. She didn't break down. There were no tears. She steeled herself, ice running through her veins, and let the anger take over.

She didn't return to her tent right away. Instead, she stayed for the next fight. A mountainous man stepped into the arena. He held a mace in one hand and an imposing broadsword hung at his waist.

A hush fell over the crowd as a spry man in black armor walked up and faced off against the larger man. Instant recognition lit in Etta's mind. He was the guard who'd chased her through the streets only the week before. If he somehow recognized her, she was as good as dead. She'd used her magic on him.

She stepped close to the wooden risers where the crowd was cheering and pressed herself into the shadows.

The man wore no helmet and his long blond hair fell freely around his handsome face. He nodded to his opponent and took up his fighting stance—bent knees. Both hands tightly gripping the hilt of his sword.

The battle began. It was strength against speed. Etta clenched her fists, at war with herself over who she wanted to win. The young man swung his sword in a graceful arc as he spun and ducked away from the mace whipping toward him. There was a beauty in the way he fought.

All movement seemed to stop in an instant. No wind. No carrying sounds. Etta narrowed her eyes. Magic. She could feel it.

The black-armored man ducked behind the barrier, waiting. The other man shifted. If he played it right, he could end this as soon as the other man came back into sight.

He stepped forward, turning to one side, just as the other man sprang out and pierced his foe where his armor failed to meet his helmet at the neck.

Etta didn't watch him go down. Her eyes were glued to the victor. His hand flicked at his side and a breeze blew through once again as if it had never stopped.

She'd seen enough. As the man went to receive his accolades from the king, Etta ducked around the corner, out of sight of the people pouring from the stands, and waited.

When he left the arena, she stepped out to block his path. His easy smile dropped at the sight of her.

"Do you recognize me?" she asked.

He nodded.

She leaned forward and dropped her voice. "I know what you can do."

A breath hissed out between his teeth.

"Come," she ordered.

He didn't argue as he followed her.

Maiya and Pierre were nowhere to be found, so they had the tent to themselves. She struggled with her mail but managed to remove it herself this time and then knelt to wash.

"What's your name?" she asked.

He hesitated.

"You know what I can do." She planted her hands on her hips. "I'm not going to turn you in."

"Edmund," he finally said.

"Feel free to remove your armor. We need to talk."

He brushed back his sweaty hair and considered her with dazzling blue eyes. Coming to a decision, he began to remove pieces of his armor, sagging in relief as he did. It took a while before he stood in front of her in only his dirty tunic and trousers.

"Now that you've seen me," she started. "Are you going to turn me in?"

He leveled her with a stare. "I would never."

Before they could go on, Maiya entered in a rush, stopping when she saw Etta's company.

"Sorry," she squeaked.

"Maiya, could you keep watch outside? I can't be interrupted." Etta pleaded with her eyes.

Maiya nodded and left them once again.

"I can keep us from being overheard," Edmund said.

Just as before in the arena, all moving air came to a halt and the noises from outside disappeared.

"That's what you did in the arena." Etta's eyes widened.

"My power isn't very strong, but I can control the winds. When I'm fighting, the only good it does me is to keep me focused. I pushed all the distractions in the crowd away, allowing me to hear every tiny movement of my opponent."

"But you're a guard. You work for the king."

He shrugged. "I was raised by a man who has no idea of my magic. He works in the palace and that has been my home for years."

"Yet now you want to be the prince's protector."

"Alex ... I mean the prince, is a good man." He closed his eyes and breathed deeply as if the words physically hurt to say. "I don't want one of those brutes by his side." He gestured in the direction of the arena.

Etta bit her lip, watching him closely. Something was off. There was something he wasn't saying. When his eyes met hers, a hint of fear sparked in them.

She shook the feeling away.

"I've been watching your fights." He scratched the back of his neck. "The king must be terrified."

"What would he have to be scared of?"

"You might just do it. He put enough men he trusted in this tournament to keep an unknown factor from coming out alive, but you're different."

Etta's mouth pressed into a flat line. To win, she'd have to kill Edmund, and something inside of her knew he could have been an ally.

Too bad they'd never get the chance to find out.

Edmund scrutinized Etta, and she wondered if he was looking for weaknesses. If both of them made it through their next fights, they would face each other in the final melee.

"Why are you here, Etta?" he asked. "Why do you want to serve the prince?"

"I don't." The words were out before she could stop them.

A growl ripped through his throat and he lunged for her, his hands holding her in place by her shirt. "Are you here to harm Alex?"

"You mean the prince who sits by his father's side while he hunts down our kind."

"You know nothing. I would lay down my life for Alexandre Durand before I let any harm come to him."

Grass started growing at his feet, but he was ready for it this time. He released her with a shove and ripped a knife from its sheath to slash at the new growth. Etta pulled her magic back, her chest heaving with heavy breaths.

His loyalty to the prince struck something in her, bringing up the same loyalty she'd once felt for the same man, only he'd been a boy still. Trying to hate that Alex was like trying to catch a single drop of rain in a storm. Impossible and overwhelming.

She despised the king and wanted nothing more than to be free of his family forever, but the boy who'd held her hand as they watched her mother's body drain of blood had never left her. He'd been the only friend she'd ever had.

Her shoulders dropped and Edmund relaxed his stance, letting his magic fade away. Sounds from outside the tent drifted in once again and the heat was pushed away by a slight breeze that lifted the flap at the entrance.

Maiya's voice rang out in surprise. "Your Majesty," she squeaked.

Etta snapped to attention and peered toward Edmund with panic in her eyes. "What is he doing here?"

Edmund shook his head. "He can't find me here. He already questions my closeness with the prince. He'll think we're conspiring."

Footsteps sounded closer, stopping right outside the tent.

"Too late," Etta whispered.

The tent flap shifted, but before anyone entered, Edmund crossed to her and pulled her against him before slamming his mouth down on hers.

Etta froze.

"Play along," Edmund whispered against her lips.

She tried to loosen her lips and brought her arms up to wrap around his neck. It wasn't an unpleasant feeling. She'd never kissed anyone before and Edmund's lips were soft and warm.

There was an amused chuckle behind them and then a throat cleared. Edmund broke away with a sheepish grin on his face. He turned to the king and bowed.

"Your Majesty." Throwing a wink to Alex behind his father, he bowed again. "My prince."

Alex didn't respond, but the king laughed again and placed a hand on Edmund's shoulder. "Celebrating, are we?"

Edmund nodded to Etta, and she gritted her teeth as she too bowed. The only reaction she got for the manly gesture was a raised eyebrow from the prince.

Edmund pulled her against his side and when she tried to protest, his grip tightened. "You know how it is, sire. Fighting riles the blood and you need to find yourself a good dame to— "

"We get the picture," Alex growled.

Etta looked between the two, noticing the curious glint in Edmund's eye and the scowl marring the prince's face.

"Go get cleaned up," the king said to Edmund. "You'll dine with us tonight, but first I need to have a talk with this girl." He turned to his son. "Alexandre, wait outside."

The prince opened his mouth as if to protest, but sighed instead and did as he was told.

Alone with the king, the hair on Etta's arms stood on end. She'd never been so close to her enemy. The congeniality from moments ago vanished and fire blazed in his eyes.

"I know who you are, girl."

The air left her chest, creating a void where feeling should live.

"I am Etta," she said. "Daughter of a farmer in the northern part of Gaule."

"You think you can lie to me?" He leaned toward her. "I am king. Viktor Basile was seen in town today."

Her heart froze. "I ..."

"I know you know the name." He narrowed his eyes. "Persinette."

Her face turned to stone as fear morphed into loathing. This man had no right to utter her name or her father's. Denial sat on the tip of her tongue, but she swallowed it back. It would do no good.

"What happens now?"

Surprise flashed across the king's face. He hadn't expected her to give in so easily. He tapped a finger against his chin. "I can't kill you. Yet. You can't just disappear from the tournament. But this is my warning to you, if you somehow survive, you will never serve my son. I know about the curse, but Alexandre will never be a part of it. Your grave is waiting, Persinette. Your wretched magic won't save you." He walked toward the door and a guard held open the flap. Without looking back, he issued one final warning. "You're being watched so I wouldn't flee if I were you."

His words shook her, fueling the rage inside her. He'd meant to sow fear, but he didn't know her. Etta did not fear death. She feared a life in chains. A life cursed.

Her hands were shaking as she left to find Pierre. She had to get a message to her father. He needed to go back to the forest.

Maiya was waiting outside and to Etta's shock, the prince stood with her.

He turned toward her with a smirk. "You did not tell me when we met that you would fight to be near me."

Etta brushed his ill-timed joke aside and looked at her friend. She grabbed her by the arm and pulled her away to tell her everything that transpired. "Find your father. He must tell mine to leave tonight."

She started running and Etta was glad for her haste. The prince was still waiting for her when she returned. He watched her expectantly.

"You would have laughed in my face." She dared him to contradict her.

"No. Something tells me you can handle yourself." He stepped closer to look at her. "You intrigue me."

"I intrigue you?"

"And worry me." He held his thumb and index finger up. "Just a tiny bit."

"Why is that?"

"Edmund is the warrior who is supposed to win this and I don't want him to die."

"Is that a threat?"

"No." He began to walk backward and spread his arms wide, a grin stretching his face. "It is not a threat, fierce Etta. It's a compliment."

His guards who'd been hidden moments before formed up around him and they were gone, leaving Etta more confused than ever. She ached to go with him, tied to him as she was. Did he feel the tug of the curse? Or was she alone in that as well?

CHAPTER 7

Alex considered the warriors who'd made it to the third round of the trials. Most had either been eliminated or fled. Five men stood before him and one woman. They were all talented, all unique. Maybe they were all even worthy of being his champion.

But only two held his interest.

He'd always thought Edmund would win. He'd never seen a man more skilled with a sword. He'd wanted him to win. The man had been with him since they were both just thirteen-year-old lads. He was the only guard brave enough to befriend the prince, to spar with him and drink with him.

But that girl. He shook his head. No, he didn't want her to kill his friend, but he didn't think he could stand to see her fall either. He was impressed she hadn't run, awed by her skill. He knew all the highborn ladies in the realm, the only ones who'd be able to afford the kind of training she'd so obviously had. But he couldn't place her.

He got the distinct impression she wanted nothing more than to make a fool of his father. To be the woman who bested his brightest fighters. To weaken him. When she looked at the king, there was something simmering beneath the surface of her blank look.

"Congratulations," Alex finally said. "You have made it this far. By today's end, only three will remain. Tomorrow there will be a final fight. Chaz and Marcus, you're up first."

He looked back to his father, who gave a nod of approval. Alex didn't want to be there. He didn't want this to be happening at all. But sometimes there was no other road.

His mother had not joined them for the day's fights, begging sickness instead. She was a kind soul, not suited for the husband she'd been given to. Even Tyson's excitement had waned after that first day. He hadn't shown up to join them and instead was probably hiding in his tunnels.

Camille was there, stone-faced as ever. Nothing rattled her.

Alex sat in the wide-backed throne next to his father and sister as the first fighters lined up across from each other. His posture feigned indifference, but he wanted nothing more than to look away.

Only, princes didn't get to hide from the things done in their name. They had to face the consequences of royalty. His hands gripped the arms of the chair as the fight began. The two were evenly matched and continued to fight until Marcus got lucky when Chaz stumbled back. Marcus arced his sword over his head, slicing through the neck of his foe.

He raised his arms in celebration.

Bile rose in Alex's throat and he swallowed it down as the body was dragged from the arena. He didn't hear the words Marcus spoke to the king as he watched Edmund walk out for his fight.

This one was much quicker and less bloody. Edmund knew how to make the killing blow in the easiest and most humane way. He didn't enjoy the fight as so many others seemed to, but he would forever do what was necessary to protect the prince. To him, that meant earning the title of champion.

He had a goodness in a palace that didn't seem to know what that meant anymore.

Alex breathed a sigh of relief as Edmund issued a single bow and left. One more for the day. But it was the one he'd been dreading the most.

When Etta walked out, the crowd roared. Commoners were fickle. She'd been a laughing stock only days ago and was now heralded as a favorite. Her golden hair rested against her mail-clad back in a braid. Two green stripes were painted across her face, giving her a feral look. She was a warrior, come to prove herself.

But as her eyes met the prince's, they narrowed. Fear gripped his chest. Was he about to see her end? He wanted to jump down to protect her, but that wasn't how this worked. And he'd seen her skill. She'd probably just quarter him instead.

A wiry fellow named Gray came to face Etta. He had at least twenty years on her. He'd trained in the mountains before the wards were in place, cutting them off from Gaule. The mountain warriors were legendary.

Etta gave the king a mocking bow and Alex heard a growl rumble in his father's chest. He glanced sideways to catch the predatory stare coming from the throne. Did his father feel threatened by a mere girl?

Gray took up a fighting stance and Etta crouched low. She closed her eyes as if needing to listen rather than see.

Alex leaned forward, pulled by some invisible force.

Gray made the first move, lunging forward. Etta spun out of the way and the two began to dance, their blades crashing together as their feet shuffled.

At first, it seemed they were evenly matched, but then Etta ran. Her feet carried her swiftly to the other side of the arena with Gray in pursuit. She took her advantage and spun on him with a jump-kick he wasn't prepared for. He flew back into the dirt and rolled aside to avoid her blade.

Jumping to his feet, he slashed his sword so quickly, she barely blocked it, and the dance began again.

It was a brilliant show.

"It's a shame," the king began. "That we can't keep them both. They'd make great additions to the guard."

Camille snorted in laughter. "You'd make her a royal guard?"

Alex ground his teeth together, unable to take his eyes from the fight.

"Camille, dear, sometimes you have to recognize talent."

A note in his father's voice sounded off, but Alex was too entranced by Etta as she kicked off the barrier and flipped. Gray was waiting for her and the next moments happened in slow motion.

Alex stood and walked to the edge of the stage before even realizing what he was doing.

The tip of Gray's sword pierced Etta's chain mail. She let out a cry and dropped to her knees, her sword falling from her grasp.

Pain shot through Alex. His heart thudded in his chest as he clutched his side that now radiated pain. His eyes found Etta again. She laid on her back, looking up at Gray as he prepared to take the final blow. He raised his sword. When he brought it down, Etta rolled to the side and whipped a knife from a sheath at her waist. Lunging up, she jabbed it into Gray's leg. He fell, screaming.

She reached for her sword and jumped to her feet before dragging it across his neck in one fluid movement.

His body stilled as his blood stained the surrounding ground.

Etta let the sword fall. Her knees buckled, and she tilted forward.

Alex, still in pain, jumped from the raised platform into the arena to sink to his knees at her side. She rolled onto her back, breathing heavily.

"I'm okay," she said, giving him a tentative smile. She'd never smiled at him before and as he pressed his hands against her shallow wound, he feared she never would again. Others ran out to help, but he didn't want to let her go.

"Your Highness," someone yelled to him. "Come away." His guards pulled him away from her as the healer arrived. They lifted him to his feet as he stood in a trance.

A young girl with caramel skin and ebony corkscrew curls peered up at him with soft eyes. "My father and I will care for her."

Edmund appeared at his side and an image of his friend kissing Etta flashed in his mind. He wanted to throw himself over her protectively.

"Alex," Edmund said into his ear. "We must leave."

The crowd pushed in and Alex finally stood.

"Are you hurt?" Edmund gestured curiously to where Alex still pressed a hand against the pain in his side.

"I ... I don't know what happened."

Edmund glanced between Etta, who was being helped to her feet, and Alex. His eyes held unspoken questions. Questions Alex wouldn't have known the answer to.

Edmund pulled him away and started toward his tent. The pain got worse with every step Alex took.

CHAPTER 8

A scream tore through Etta's chest as she was carried through the camp. Pierre laid her down on the small pallet in her tent and another shock of pain jolted her.

Instinct had her pressing a hand to her side. It came away sticky with blood. Pushing her breath past her clenched teeth, she stared up at the ceiling. One. Two. Three.

Dammit, counting was no help.

She couldn't picture the moment Gray died. Everything after she was stabbed became a blur of motion. Maybe that was a mercy. She'd seen and done enough in the last couple days to haunt her for a lifetime.

This was not her. She'd spent her life training to be a protector. Not a killer. Maybe they were one and the same?

"Ahhh." She clutched the edges of the pallet, rocked by dizziness, as everything went fuzzy before her eyes.

"Breathe, Etta." Maiya's calm voice came closer as she knelt down. "You're going to be fine."

"Easy for you to say. You don't have to fight again tomorrow with your guts spilling out of your side."

Maiya smiled. Smiled! Etta wanted to strangle her. The pain sent bolts of anger through her mind.

Etta groaned as Maiya began to remove her mail shirt.

"This is going to hurt," she said. "But I need you to raise your arms."

Etta screamed as her skin pulled where she'd been wounded, but she managed to raise her arms enough for Maiya to wrestle off her mail and the shirt beneath it, leaving Etta with only the cloth she'd used to bind her breasts for the fight.

Maiya ran a soft hand over the planes of Etta's stomach, sending pulses of warmth into her skin. The pain began to abate. She closed her eyes when her fingers found the edges of the gash. The skin began to stitch together. Etta stared in amazement as her wound healed. When it was closed, all that remained was the blood streaking across her skin.

Maiya opened her eyes and pulled back her hand. "I'm going to leave the bruising. If anyone asks, that is what felled you, but the sword only nicked your clothing."

Etta sat up and stared at her friend. "Your magic is so much more useful than mine."

Maiya laughed, getting to her feet. "One day there will be use for all of it."

Before Etta could respond, Pierre's voice sounded outside. "Your Highness, you can't just go in there."

Apparently, a prince doesn't have to listen because he barged in moments later and froze, his eyes finding Etta. "You're okay."

"Of course I am," she snapped.

His eyes widened as he took her in and then Edmund joined them.

"Etta," Maiya whispered, gesturing to her lack of clothing.

Etta scrambled for her shirt, only realizing how much blood was soaked into it when she put it on.

"Whose blood is that?" Alex demanded.

"Obviously not mine." Etta stood up as if to prove she was fine but stumbled.

"But I saw him stab you."

"Your eyes deceive you, Your Highness. Or maybe they just show you what you want to see."

"What's that supposed to mean?"

"You're an educated man. Think about it." She picked up her mail and carried it to the basin of water to clean it. "Tell me, my prince, do you visit all of your warriors?"

"I ... I just came to see if you'd be withdrawing or fighting tomorrow."

"I don't withdraw." She dropped the mail and turned to face him. "I'm going to win. You can tell your father he bet against the wrong girl."

"My father?"

"And when I win, I won't be so easy to get rid of. Tell him he doesn't need to send his son to keep me in line. Because it won't work. I don't bow down to threats."

Confusion crossed the prince's face, but she didn't believe for a second that he wasn't in his father's inner circle.

Edmund glanced between the two nervously. Her victory would mean his failure.

Alex opened his mouth to speak, then thought better of it. Where were the jokes or pretty smiles he was known for? Gone. Cool aloofness sat in their place as he turned on his heel and left the tent.

Edmund hesitated, his eyes finding Maiya. He pointed to her in question and Etta nodded.

"So you were stabbed?" He rubbed his chin. "In the very same place Alex had pains."

"Out with it, Edmund," Etta said.

"Be careful."

He followed the prince and Etta went back to cleaning her mail in silence.

They made a show of the final fight. It was entertainment on its grandest stage. Etta stretched her muscles as she stood off to the side of the arena. Her entire body ached from three days of fighting men who were at least twice her size. But she'd made it. Her father would be proud.

She scanned the crowd of their own accord as they'd done before every fight, looking for his familiar face. The rational part of her hoped he'd fled after her warning about the king. It wasn't safe.

She'd barely thought about what would happen beyond this fight. The king said he wouldn't let her become champion. Would Alex have any say? Would he want her after she'd killed his man?

Her eyes found Edmund's. He gave her a toothy grin, seemingly unfazed by the events about to unfold.

Loud, booming drums beat slow and steady. One. Two. Three. One. Two. Three. One. Two. Three. The rhythm was punctuated by chants from the crowd.

Banners waved in the breeze. Would Edmund use his powers today? She wished more than anything she could use hers.

The three competitors had already been introduced. Edmund was the favorite, loved by the king and the people alike, with his brilliant smile, easy charm, and deadly skill. Etta was the underdog, beloved and hated at the same time. Ward, the third competitor, was the villain. He was a hulking brute with a pox-marked face and a snarl on his lips.

Together, they represented the three tenants of a good warrior. Cunning. Speed. And strength.

They were about to see which one of those prevailed.

Edmund walked toward her, all hint of a smile gone from his lips. He looked at her somberly and bowed his head to speak softly. "I'm sorry we met this way."

"This wasn't how we met."

He barked out a laugh that was devoid of humor. "Then I'm sorry this is how we end."

Something cracked inside of her. "Are you afraid?"

"Yes."

"I think I've always been afraid."

"Fear is a part of life when you are a child of the kingdom of Bela."

She reached for his hand and gave it one quick squeeze. "Forgive me for what I have to do today."

He nodded. "We do what we must. I only wanted the chance to protect Alex. If I am not the victor, promise me you will never leave his side. He is a good man surrounded by bad people."

She studied him for a long moment. His loyalty was constant, unwavering. She envied him. Dipping her head, she uttered, "I promise."

He blew out a breath. "We would have been great friends, you and I."

"If we weren't fated to kill each other."

"Fate has nothing to do with this. Only a king with a thirst for blood."

He backed away after giving her a glimpse into the man she was about to fight. A man who hated the king, but loved his son.

She fingered the knife in a sheath on her wrist and then felt for the solid weight of her sword.

Edmund walked into the arena first, twirling a spear, much to the delight of the crowd. He waved to them and smiled wide.

Ward lumbered after him, carrying a heavy iron sword and spear.

Etta was last. The stands shook as people stomped in time with the drums.

They quieted when the king stood. "Today we will name my son's protector. These three before me have battled the best warriors in the kingdom to be standing in for the final fight. Three enter, only one will survive. They fight for all of us, for the protection of Gaule, and for your prince."

Alex gripped the arms of his chair and leaned forward anxiously. Etta knew he'd be wishing for her death. Only then would his friend survive.

"Warriors," the king shouted. "We will honor you in death. Take your places."

The three formed a triangle. Etta bent her knees, ready for an immediate attack. The king raised a hand. When he dropped it, the fight could begin.

Ward charged first, going after Etta, the perceived weakest competitor. She spun out of the way and his sword hit nothing but air.

The noise around them dimmed and Etta glanced briefly at Edmund. He gave no indication that he was using magic.

Ward came at her again and Edmund jumped into the fight. His sword blocked Ward's swing, and they locked in a struggle of strength. Etta circled around behind Ward, but he spun, kicking a foot back to catch Edmund in the stomach. He went down hard.

Etta ducked another arc of his sword as he brought it down with one hand, his other gripping his spear. He jabbed it toward her and she jumped back. Then it became a battle of his strength verse her speed. He threw his spear aside so he could wrap a second hand around the hilt of his sword.

Etta swung out wide, using her sword to block his, as she turned to kick her leg out. Her foot collided with his stomach, but he barely budged.

Then Edmund was back. For a few moments, it was as if they were on the same side, both against Ward. Ward jabbed his sword toward Etta, catching it in her mail, but unable to plunge it in further as in that moment, Edmund made a killing blow. He pierced Ward's armor and jammed his sword in as far as it could go. Ward stumbled back and Edmund jumped out of the way. The sizable man went down, twitched once, and then fell still.

Etta stared at Edmund for a moment, her chest heaving. He shoved a hand through his sweaty blond hair. Neither wanted to make the first move. Edmund's sword was stuck in Ward. He lunged for his spear, spinning it between his hands. She'd seen him fight before. She'd never get past his spear with a knife. Her sword could knock it away with ease, but if she was forced to fight a man she respected, at least she'd make it a fair fight.

She dropped her sword, eying him to see if he'd make a grab for it. He didn't.

Walking toward Ward's discarded spear, she leaned down slowly.

Just like training. She breathed in. A spear was nothing more than a staff with an iron tip. She'd complained to her father about the hours they spent fighting with a useless weapon, but now it might be the thing that saved her life.

Issuing a short prayer of thanks to her father, she turned and faced Edmund. His expression was grim, his face dripping with sweat.

There was no one there but the two of them. Nothing but their spears.

Etta held the weapon aloft, waiting.

Edmund struck first, using his spear as she was, ignoring the pointed tip. She blocked him easily, pushing him back on his heels.

They slashed at each other, their weapons cracking together. It was the only sound either of them could hear other than their own frantic breathing. Edmund's cloak of stillness continued to hang around them. She searched for any sign of distraction in him, but he used his magic as if it was just another part of his battle plan.

He jabbed, and she spun to hit it away before cracking her spear against his back as her father had done so many times to her.

He didn't go down. He turned to face her once more, and she leaped, delivering a swift kick to his torso. He fell, rolling as he did before popping up once again. His style mixed strength with quick feet. A deadly combination. The thought struck her that maybe Edmund deserved to become the prince's champion. He was loyal and brave and skilled.

The one thing he wasn't was cursed. He was tied to the prince by love, not magic.

But she didn't want to die. And the only way for Edmund to win was with her death.

She dove into the fight more avidly than before. Every strike of his was blocked, every move anticipated.

This was not how she ended, a puppet of the king.

Edmund slowed as exhaustion took hold and Etta pressed on. Something inside her told her Edmund would win any battle against the great Viktor Basile.

His magic allowed him to concentrate, but it was no real advantage.

His advantage had been that he was fighting for something he believed in.

Well, she was fighting for a greater reason than that. Revenge. Hatred. Because she had no other choice.

He went for her stomach and she grabbed his staff, throwing hers to the ground, and twisted. His fingers held fast until she jerked it back toward him, jabbing him in the stomach. The breath was knocked from his lungs and he fell back, releasing her.

Etta spun the spear around, angling the tip at Edmund's chest where he lay panting on the ground. She met his eyes. He deserved that much.

The sounds of the crowd began to close in around them once again.

Etta narrowed her eyes in question.

"If I'm to die," Edmund explained. "I don't want it to be in silence."

He raised his chin, ready to face his fate. His words from earlier entered her mind. *Fate has nothing to do with this. Only a king with a thirst for blood.*

Etta put a foot on Edmund's chest to keep him down and raised her gaze to the king. He stood on his platform, gripping the rail in front of him in anticipation. Edmund was a favorite, but that didn't mean the king's desire for a gruesome ending was any less.

Etta's chest ached, her stomach churning with disgust. This wasn't her. She didn't kill good people. Her hands had too much blood on them already.

"What are you waiting for?" someone in the crowd yelled.

"Kill!" another screamed.

"Finish this," the king finally commanded.

He met her stare, a smirk turning up one corner of his mouth. She knew that if she made this kill, no one would be leaving this fight alive. The king made it very clear she would never be champion.

"Etta," Edmund said, his voice quivering. "I'm ready."

"I'm not," she whispered.

She lowered the spear as the crowd howled in disappointment.

"I'm not going to kill you, Edmund."

Relief flooded his face, mixed with confusion.

She leaned down, extending a hand. "What's the point?"

He clasped her hand and hauled himself to his feet. "I don't know if you're really stupid, or really brave." He jerked his head toward the king who was climbing from his platform. The royal guards entered the arena. "He won't let this happen."

Etta shrugged. "What's done is done."

The guards marched toward them first, followed by the king. They surrounded Etta and Edmund, their swords drawn.

Etta's hands were shaking. She felt pressure on one of them and glanced down to see Edmund holding it.

Alex joined his father in front of them. He stared at Edmund and Etta's clasped hands with a furrowed brow, but it was covered with the pure relief on his face to have Edmund alive.

"Guards," the king ordered. "Restrain her."

A strong grip ripped Etta from Edmund.

"No," Alex protested.

His father turned to him. "Son, it is time I tell you and everyone else who this girl really is."

Etta bucked and kicked against the guards as they took her knife and held her arms in their iron holds.

"People of Gaule," the king raised his voice, facing the confused crowd. "Etta -"

His words were cut off as an arrow flew toward him, embedding its shaft in his throat. Chaos erupted as the crowd tried to get as far away as possible while their king crumpled to the ground, blood gurgling from his lips.

Etta was released as the guards ran toward their dying ruler. Alex dropped down beside him, holding his head in his lap. He looked up at the guards and pointed.

"It came from that way. Go."

Three of them ran off to find the attacker.

Edmund joined his friend, but Etta couldn't move.

Then she heard her name. "Etta! Etta!" Maiya ran across the arena. "It's your father. You must come now."

The king forgotten, Etta streaked after her friend, her protesting muscles not enough to stop her from getting to her father's side.

CHAPTER 9

Pierre hovered over her father when Etta arrived. He'd collapsed near a crop of trees on the far side of the arena. People stopped to gawk, but Pierre held them back.

Etta crashed to her knees as her father tried to lift his head.

"Persinette," he whispered.

She leaned closer and took his hand. "I'm here, Father."

"Persinette, the King knew of your magic." He let his head fall back. "I was cursed to protect him, but I chose. You can choose. Protecting you was more important."

Etta's gaze snagged on the familiar bow laying nearby. She looked back to her father, shaking her head as tears poured down her cheeks. No blood stained his skin, but in the same spot where he'd shot the king, Viktor's skin glowed red.

Etta put a hand on her father's chest and bent her head. "Your curse is broken now, Father."

He smiled weakly.

"Etta." Maiya appeared at her side. "The prince comes."

"Find another way to break your curse, Persinette." Her father heaved a wet sigh. "I was wrong. You can't live your life chained to them. You've always been meant for more." They were the words she'd longed to hear during their many hours of training. She'd wanted to know he believed in her. Only at the end could he truly see.

As the guard's footsteps came closer, Etta scrambled to her feet and wiped her face. Prince Alexandre's guards pushed through the crowd and then he was there with Edmund at his side.

Alex took in the sight of her father and his eyes widened.

Her father stared back at the prince.

"Viktor Basile," Alex said under his breath as if his name were a curse.

His red eyes were the only indication that his father had just died.

Alex stepped closer before turning to look at Etta. "Already doing good work for me, Etta. I see you found my father's killer."

"I am sorry for your loss, Your Highness." Etta stepped back and lowered her head to hide her tears.

To her surprise, Alex crouched down next to her father and put a hand on his shoulder. "It's been a long time, Viktor."

Bile rose in Etta's throat. She wanted to demand the prince stop touching him. It wasn't his right. The Durands ruined her family, killed her mother, and now even took her father.

And yet, they still held the noose around her neck. They just didn't know it.

Alex didn't ask Viktor why he did it. He knew. They all did. Viktor Basile was the man who'd protected them from La Dame and been hunted as a reward. He'd been the king's greatest friend turned most horrifying nightmare.

"Is the king dead?" Etta's father asked, his voice fading.

Alex nodded.

He closed his eyes. "Then I am free."

His body shuddered as he took one final breath and then went still.

Alex bowed his head, and a cry broke free of Etta. She stumbled forward as the ground beneath her feet began to shake. A groan tore through the earth. Townsfolk began to run as the hastily built arena nearby broke apart and crumbled.

The guards shoved Alex ahead and his eyes darted around frantically as Etta watched the world fall apart around them.

"Camille!" Alex yelled.

Edmund grabbed Etta's arm, jolting her from her frozen state.

Camille limped over. "What's happening?"

Etta reached out with her magic, letting it course through her body. Her magic forged a connection between herself and the natural world around her. She could feel the pain of the earth. The way the ground ripped apart, shrieking in agony at the death of her father. And then it struck her. Eyes flashing open wide, she gasped. "The wards!" She dodged a rock surging toward her head. "They're coming down!"

Understanding dawned in Edmund's eyes. A person's magic died with them. If Viktor Basile was dead, his magic couldn't hold the wards. If the wards were gone, there was no protection against La Dame.

Etta searched frantically for Maiya and Pierre, but they were nowhere to be found.

"You're coming with us," Alex said, taking his frightened horse from a guard.

"I'm not going anywhere with you." She fell back.

"Etta." She jumped at Edmund's touch. "You won the tournament. Your place is at the palace now."

Her eyes flicked to her father's still form, and she held back the tears that built in her eyes. If her connection to Viktor Basile was known… she shook her head. Her father killed the king.

She searched Alex's face for any sign of his own distress. She may hate the Durands, but she wasn't heartless.

He looked too stunned to process it.

Edmund flung out a jolt of calming wind to the horses, noticeable only to Etta. He climbed on behind Camille. Alex mounted his horse extended a hand down to Etta. She didn't have time to think before she accepted the help and wrapped her arms around his waist.

They rode as fast as the horses could take them. The guards were left behind to try to find and calm the remaining horses.

Tents collapsed in on themselves as they galloped by. Panicked people ran to avoid the falling structures. The ride to the palace was a thunderous pursuit of hooves and fallen debris. The gates stood open when they arrived and they raced through. They didn't slow as they passed through the outer castle and bypassed the stables entirely, making for the inner palace gate instead. Once inside the courtyard, the rumbling began to calm, and the ground stopped shaking.

Etta bent over to catch her breath and they slid from their horses.

Camille paced back and forth, her cane echoing across the stone courtyard. She stopped every few feet to shoot a glare at Etta.

"We should get inside," Edmund said softly.

Neither of the royal children responded, stunned as they were by the day's events.

Tyson came barreling across the courtyard. "What's going on? Are you okay?" He caught sight of Etta. "You won? I knew you would. I bet on it with a few of my guards."

Edmund cleared his throat and Tyson turned his way.

"Edmund." He beamed, walking forward to slap him on the back. "I didn't mean that I wanted her to beat you ... wait, how are you both here?"

"Father is dead," Camille wailed suddenly. She pointed one long finger at Etta. "And it's all her fault." She stomped inside, leaving the rest of them in shock.

Alex's eyes clouded with anger and he set his jaw.

"Alex?" Tyson asked.

"Father is dead." He turned to his brother. "But make no mistake, it was no one's fault but his own and now Gaule is once again at the mercy of magic."

Tyson opened his mouth in question and then shut it.

"Did you feel it?" Edmund asked. "The wards are gone."

Alex shook his head and walked up the steps as a host of guards and servants descended upon him. He waved them off, but they wouldn't be deterred. "I'm fine," he bellowed, marching past them.

They turned their attention to Tyson, ignoring Etta and Edmund entirely. The young prince didn't cry, although he looked like he wanted to. The boy who was known for his easy smile and bright eyes had dulled.

With the wards now gone, Etta wondered what the coming months would take from all of them.

She was luckier than most. She had nothing left to lose.

"What do you mean the wards are gone?" The portly Lord Leroy yelled, his voice echoing around the council chamber.

The room was purely ornamental since no council had been in use in the years of protection under the wards. But Lord Leroy held a high status with Alexandre's father. He was already trying to exert his influence with the new king.

Duchess Moreau put a hand on his shoulder to calm his pacing and turned to the prince who would soon be a prince no more.

"Your Highness." Warmth flowed from her voice. "Are you certain?"

Alexandre's father's voice filtered through his mind. One of his many lessons. *Never trust the Moreaus. The Duchess will manipulate your sword straight through your back.*

Gaule had a long tradition of keeping enemies close to the crown, but he had trouble seeing her as an enemy. The Moreaus controlled vast swaths of lands and towns near the border. The Moreaus had a long history of protecting magic folk. That in itself was a good enough reason not to trust them, but there were so few people he could trust. He shook her hand off his arm and stepped back to gain some distance.

Alex glanced around the cavernous room. It was a good place to have private conversations with advisers, but it only made him feel inadequate for the position he was now forced to take. It should have been his father dealing with broken wards and advisers.

A week had passed since that sickening moment in the arena when his father crumpled to the ground as if he wasn't the most powerful man in Gaule.

Then again, maybe he wasn't. Not when Viktor Basile lived.

Now they were both dead. Gone.

And he had a kingdom to run.

"I've sent an exploratory force to the border to see about the wards. That's why I haven't called on you until now. The unit I sent was due back yesterday." The prince scrubbed a hand across his face. "There was substantial damage from the quakes. I've put a few units to work in town to make repairs. I've sent others to the towns farther out from the palace to see how they have fared as well." He turned toward the door. "Now, you are informed and I must see about finding my men."

He turned to go but Lord Leroy called him back. "Your majesty, we must plan a coronation."

Alex sighed. He knew the duke was right. "My father is not even in the ground. Coronate me if you must, but no ceremony."

No one argued.

"And your protector?"

"What about her?" he snapped.

"She won the tournament, but it was non-binding. There has been no ceremony yet. With your father now ..."

"Dead?"

"Yes, well, you could choose a protector who projects a certain image. A certain strength."

He narrowed his eyes. "And with him gone, I could also choose an adviser with half a brain."

Lord Leroy reeled back.

"I am not legally bound to accept Etta as my protector, but she has won the tournament. I will not tarnish my honor or that of this crown by lowering the worth of my father's word. If the position is symbolic, let it symbolize the strength of our character. Besides, she bested some of our most accomplished men in combat. I'd say she's more than capable."

He walked from the room with heavy steps. He couldn't remember the last time he slept or ate, but there were more pressing matters. Edmund and his men were missing. He'd sent them to the border the day following the quakes and expected them back yesterday.

If this worry was what it meant to be king, he wished he'd been born a pauper.

As soon as the thought entered his mind, he knew it wasn't right. His entire life, all he'd wanted to do was protect his people. He'd been raised to think that meant keeping magic from their lands, but if the wards were gone, only magic could replace them. He wouldn't know where to start.

Captain Anders fell in step beside him, giving a slight incline of his head.

"Do you have to follow me?" Alex asked tiredly.

"Sire, I know you had your own guards who gave you more ... space before, but you are to be king now and must be guarded more closely."

"By the captain of the guard?" He raised an eyebrow.

Anders grunted, a scowl crossing his face. It wasn't what he wanted to be doing, but he'd do his duty. Anders was good for that. As long as you didn't try to get a conversation out of him and could live on snarls, he'd do. It wasn't like Alex minded. He hadn't been one for talking in the past week.

"I'll have a personal guard selected by week's end, assuming Edmund returns by then."

"No. My son is not suited to guard the king. You have more tested soldiers to consider."

Alex stopped abruptly and turned toward the tall man. His broad shoulders and blond hair were the only things he had in common with his son. He raised Edmund on his own, but where Edmund was quick to smile, Anders was eternally sour. Anders rose through the ranks, gaining the trust of Alex's father, but maybe it was time for the captain of the guard to be a man Alex trusted.

"Captain," Alex said coldly. "Your battle-tested men failed my father."

Anders' face blanched.

Alex held up a hand. "I do not hold them to account. But the next time you try to give me an order, you will find yourself with no men to lead."

Was any of it going to get any easier? He started walking without waiting for an answer. Anders followed without a word, his heavy steps sounding against the stones beneath his feet.

Before he knew it, Alex found himself heading toward Etta's room. His steps faltered. He hadn't been able to face her since arriving back at the palace. Officially, he'd been too busy. Unofficially, she barely knew him and had been the one person who seemed to see straight through his facade. Unable to deal with more changes, he'd given the task of her well-being to Camille, but she was to be his protector and it was time he looked her in the eye. As protector, she might have no real role, but she'd be with him always. The thought soothed him. Maybe that was the point of a protector—so the king didn't have to be so alone in ruling.

"Was it really Viktor?" Anders asked.

Alex hid is surprise at the blunt question. He'd almost forgotten Anders was there.

When Alex nodded, Anders' eyes darkened. "That man was dangerous from the first time he set foot in this palace. I told your father that many times, but ..." He shook his head.

"But the man was his closest friend." Alex gave him an icy look. He wanted to despise the man who killed his father, but part of him remembered the Viktor who tried to teach him how to wield a sword. He'd spent more time with Viktor and his daughter than he had with his own father.

"Evil is what he was. He had the magic."

Alex couldn't disagree with that sentiment. None of them were safe when magic ran rampant in the kingdom.

Geoff was sitting outside Etta's door, dozing off, when they arrived. Anders stopped in front of him and kicked at his legs. Geoff awoke with a start.

"What are you doing here, Geoff?" Alex asked.

Geoff wasn't quick enough to hide his scowl. He hadn't forgiven Alex and Tyson for knocking him out before the tournament.

"The princess put me here," he snarled. "I'm to keep anyone from going in or out."

"My God, man." Alex shoved him aside. "You mean to tell me we've been keeping her locked in her rooms?"

"Princess Camille's orders." He shrugged.

"Go back to my sister and tell her I demand her presence in the throne room first thing in the morning." He paid no more attention to the guard as he knocked on the door.

"I told you, I'm not hungry," an angry voice yelled from inside.

"Etta, it is Prince Alexandre. May I come in?"

"No."

"Please. I must speak to you."

He heard her stomp across the room moments before the door cracked open. "Come to check on my prison cell, Your Highness?"

Her eyes were red as if she'd been crying, but all tears were dry as her pupils blazed when she met his gaze. She shifted her eyes to the guard and scanned Anders from head to toe.

He stared with open distaste.

He didn't know why, but it caused Alex's anger to rise.

"Anders," he snapped. "Show your respect to the woman who saved your son's life."

Anders' jaw clenched as he bent at the waist for the slightest of bows. Alex pushed down his irritation. It wouldn't do to make an enemy of the captain of the guard.

"Your son would be ...?" Etta asked.

"Edmund." Alex scratched his cheek.

Etta's cheeks reddened. "Oh."

Oh? What the hell did that even mean? Did their kiss mean more than Alex thought? He'd had his reasons for believing it to be a ruse. But then what was Edmund doing there that day?

"Anders," Alex ordered. "Leave us."

"But, Your Highness ..."

"My new protector is not going to kill me. Out."

The door thudded behind him, locking them in a silent stand-off. Etta's eyes flitted around the room, anywhere but at him. She turned and walked back to busy herself straightening the blankets on the bed in the center of the room. Directly next to her, silver moonlight streamed in through a three paned window, framed in gold. The moonlight illuminated her strong features.

"I didn't order you to be locked in here," he finally said.

She didn't look at him. "Does it matter who gave the order? I'm still a prisoner."

"You're not." He stepped toward her. "I promise."

"Your promises mean nothing to me."

She sniffled and sat on the edge of her bed.

"Are you okay?" he asked.

"Am I okay?" A laugh pushed past her lips, but it sounded wrong somehow. "What does that mean? Are any of us okay?

Your father just died, thrusting you onto the throne. You're not okay, but you must look like you are." She rested her elbows on her knees. "I ... lost someone close to me recently and I have no way to mourn him. My hands have been bathed in blood on the command of the crown I now must serve." She finally met his stare. "Have you ever killed anyone, Prince?"

When he shook his head, she continued. "No, you wouldn't have. You give the order for people to die, but you never have to feel their life seep out. For a moment it feels good. There's a kind of power in taking a life. But that power comes at a cost. Each kill breaks apart the soul."

She gestured to the door. "That man out there would have lost his son if I'd have obeyed your father. So, your Highness, I will serve you. I'll give my soul. But if you ever again ask me if I'm okay, I'll break that pretty face of yours."

CHAPTER 10

The next morning, Etta's dress dragged along the ground as she trailed the prince and Anders through the labyrinth that made up the palace. She stepped on the hem, catching herself before pitching forward and uttering a curse. Camille provided her with a few worn dresses belonging to one of the servants. None of them were truly her size, but the princess didn't seem to care.

Her icy demeanor fit much better with Etta's opinion of the Durands than Alex's flirtations or Tyson's more youthful exuberance. The princess had it in for Etta.

Being inside the palace again had Etta's skin crawling with nerves. Since leaving when she was young, it had represented an enemy, a fear. Now it was supposed to be her home.

Alex demanded she accompany him to a meeting in the throne room. She'd be at his side for every meeting going forward. Alex would be her constant companion. She didn't hate the idea, and then she hated herself for not hating it.

Keeping those two ideas in her mind kept her sane in an insane world.

They turned yet another corner and Etta made note of every step she took. It was a habit instilled by her ever-cautious father. Notice everything. Forget nothing. Know your surroundings. Plan an escape route.

She could use his wise counsel or even his stern teachings right about now, but she'd cried too many tears for him. Alex seemed unaffected by his own father's death. How much of that was just him playing the act of prince? Camille burst into tears every few minutes when she wasn't scolding some poor soul, and Tyson had disappeared altogether.

A group of onlookers waited in the throne room for their first audience with the prince since the king's death. He barely glanced at them. His focus stayed on his sister who stood on the platform next to the throne as if she too would rule.

Anders put a hand on Etta's arm to hold her back as Alex walked up and stared at the throne. More than a few people sucked in their breaths. Was he going to sit in it? So soon after his father's death? His shoulders tensed as he took the steps slowly and then turned, fanning his cloak around him, and sat.

His face held no emotion, but his posture was rigid.

Was this the moment? Etta wondered. She didn't know why Alex insisted she come when they hadn't yet done the ceremony making her official, but she'd been waiting for someone, anyone, to reveal her identity. Could it be possible that the king hadn't told anyone who she really was?

Alex swept a measured gaze across the room and she breathed deeply, positioning herself for easy access to the door.

But his next statement wasn't about her at all.

"Camille," he snapped, gesturing her down off the platform.

Camille's face went slack, but she obeyed, stepping down to stand in front of him.

"Tell me why you've had my protector locked up."

"I ... I..." she stuttered before straightening up and brushing a hand down the front of her blue lace dress. "Father didn't trust her."

Alex leaned forward and lowered his voice. Etta waited.

"Father didn't trust anyone."

Camille's mouth dropped open. "You would speak ill of a man who has not yet been buried?"

"It is those alive who are important now. We have bigger problems than Father not wanting a woman by my side."

"Are you so blinded by her beauty that you can't see something isn't right?"

"Beauty has nothing to do with it." He raised his voice so those at the back of the room could hear. "My protector has won the tournament and I will honor her victory. There will be consequences for those who try to interfere again."

People murmured, but none had the courage, or stupidity, to voice their concerns aloud. Instead, they cast suspicious glances toward Etta.

Camille turned her back on her brother.

"I did not dismiss you," Alex growled.

She turned back toward him, her eyes an unforgiving cool. "You are not my king yet, Brother."

She spun and snapped her cane against the floor as she marched away. As she passed Etta, she said, "My father knew something about you and I'm going to figure out what it was."

When she left, Alex removed himself from the throne, ignoring the others who wished to speak with him. As he walked to Anders, he scratched the back of his neck. "I hated that."

"That girl is very much like your father," Anders said.

Alex ignored the way the captain referred to the princess, but the reverence in his tone did not pass his notice. Giving Anders a long look, Alex spun on his heel and marched from the throne room—the seat of his new power—weighed down with the responsibility of a kingdom.

Etta left conflicted. The Durands had destroyed generations of her family. She wasn't there by choice. But with each word out of the prince's mouth, the edges of her hate began to crumble. She worried that once that was gone, all she'd have was utter emptiness.

Plush comfort surrounded Etta. After living in a shabby cabin in the Black Forest, how could her circumstances have changed so drastically?

Sleepy thoughts drifted through her mind as the morning sun lit her face. Her eyes took in the oversized canopy bed with silky fabric draped from high above. It was heavenly. An aroma filled the air, cinnamon tendrils dancing below her nose.

She bolted upright as her mind cleared and she realized where she was. The palace. Her new home. The sweet smell from before turned her stomach as she set bare feet onto the woolly carpet surrounding the bed. Soft fibers gave way to chilled stone as she walked toward the sitting area that consisted of a sofa, two chairs, and a fireplace that went unused during the summer months.

A tray sat on the table before one of the chairs, piled high with various pastries and a pot of tea. Another familiar smell stabbed through her awareness and she lunged for a covered dish, pulling the lid free. Bacon.

Her father would bring bacon home from the market when he went to town, and it was her favorite food, not because it was delicious—even though it was—but because it meant he'd returned safely. And that he'd remembered her while he was away.

He never ate any of it.

She closed her eyes to keep the tears from flowing as she chewed her way through each glorious piece. She'd barely eaten the day before and her stomach protested so much activity.

Ten days. He'd been dead for ten days now. And she still didn't know what her role at the castle was to be. A knock sounded from her door and she jumped to her feet to run toward her wardrobe for a shift to cover her nakedness. Nightgowns tangled in her legs when she twisted in her sleep. Only when her father was home did she wear them.

Opening the door, she blinked in surprise, recognizing the queen standing before her.

Recovering from her momentary stupor, she dipped. "Your Majesty."

"Oh, my dear," the queen said warmly, holding out her arms that were piled high with clothing. "Help an old lady out."

"You aren't old, Madame."

A wide smile spread across her face. "If I wanted constant compliments, I'd spend my days with the highborn chirpers in their sewing rooms."

Etta stepped back, and the queen rushed into the room, her sapphire blue, silk dress swishing about her legs. Etta stared. When the wards had been in place, certain trade items like silk weren't coming into the kingdom. They'd only had access to the goods that were made in Gaule, becoming self-sustaining. That would change now.

The queen set her pile of clothes on the bed and followed Etta's sightline with a laugh. "Do you like it? I had it made from some old drapes that were in my room. Hideous drapes, but they made a gorgeous dress."

Etta just shook her head. The queen was not often seen outside of the palace and this was not what she'd been expecting.

"Do you speak, girl?" she asked with a laugh.

Etta coughed. "Yeah, I mean yes, my lady. It's an honor to meet you."

"Me? You're the woman who just beat the kingdom's best fighting men in combat." She leaned in. "I was probably the only one in the palace actually rooting for you." She winked. "Although, I couldn't watch. It was just dreadful. I abhor violence. And that tournament was unnecessary."

"I am ..." Etta cleared her throat. "I'm sorry how it ended."

Sadness swam in the queen's eyes for a moment before she shut them and breathed deeply. "One good man died that day. And one monster." She opened them and pierced Etta with a look that cut straight through her.

Their eyes met, and some meaning passed through their connection, but Etta broke it before the queen saw too deeply.

"Anyway." She brightened and in an instant, all trace of sadness was gone. "I heard you could use some clothes."

Etta held the laugh that escaped her as she walked back to her wardrobe and opened the door. Yesterday's dress hung in the front, but the entire bottom hem had been slashed with a knife. "If I'm going to protect the king, I need to be able to walk without falling on my face."

Queen Catrine's answering laugh bounced off the high ceilings. "That you are. It would have been easier if you'd have been able to gather your belongings from your tent, but alas ..."

"I didn't need anything in that tent." Her only possessions that mattered were the sword resting against the wall, the mail shirt on the chair, and the knife hidden underneath the mattress of the bed for easy access.

The queen pressed her lips together. "Well, find something in that pile to wear. I must return to my rooms for a dull tea with Lady Leroy. She will busy my ear with worries about her equally dull daughters." Her sigh was exaggerated. "You'll get to know them soon enough. Her eldest, Amalie, is betrothed to my Alexandre."

Etta jerked her head up before looking away suddenly to hide her curiosity. No doubt she'd have to protect this highborn priss who was to be queen. What kind of woman would they marry to the king?

The queen continued talking, unaware of the questions rolling through Etta's mind. "Tonight you have an invitation to dine in the king's rooms."

"I do?" Protect, yes. Attend meetings, sure. Follow the king around, she'd survive. But socializing with him? Dining with him? Was every part of her life to be dictated by the curse?

"He'll send someone to retrieve you."

Alone again, Etta rifled through the clothing, trying to get her mind off the impending dinner and the future queen. Simple trousers and tunics made up the lot, and she'd never been more thankful for clothes. As she pulled a pair of black pants from the pile, a scrap of paper fluttered through the air.

Her fingers snatched it before it hit the ground.

If you are in need of a friend, look to the stables.

-Edmund

Why would Edmund send her to the stables when he wasn't even here? The first time she'd ever met Edmund flashed in her mind—the day she'd left him tied up in an alley. Her heart rate picked up. *Vérité*.

She pulled on the pants and a shortened white smock with a hood before stepping into her boots and lacing them up. They still had dried blood spattered on them from the tournament, but they were the best she could do.

Walking to the door, she ran her fingers through her hair to untangle the knots and pulled up her hood. The awful guard no longer sat outside her door, but that room would never be more than a prison. As she hurried away, freedom bloomed within her.

The walk was familiar. Wood paneled halls, adorned with pastel paintings and golden archways. The guards at the palace doors paid her no mind as she pushed out into the bright sun. It'd been over a week since she experienced its warmth on her face. She was used to being outdoors for all things except sleep. But life in the forest seemed like a faraway dream now.

She closed her eyes to soak in the moment but was brought back to reality when a man carrying two buckets of water bumped into her, splashing it across her stomach. Her eyes snapped open, and she scowled, but he'd already moved on.

"Wonderful," she muttered as she marched through the courtyard and out into the lifeblood of the castle: the people. Houses lined the streets, each one looking like the home she'd tried so hard to forget. They backed up against the inner wall, crowded together like the petals of a dying bud with no room to breathe.

The gate to the outer part of the castle stood open, but she knew it could be closed at a moment's notice. She'd seen it happen before. When she was ten, a group of men and women used magic to terrorize the outer castle. They'd closed the inner gate to protect the royal family. She could still hear the screams.

That was the first time she knew not all magic was good.

The outer castle was like a town in itself, crowded and bustling with activity. She avoided the most familiar places and went directly to the stables. There, nothing had changed in the years that passed. A wooden structure that had seen better days was surrounded by a pen in which horses wandered about. It was closed off by a fence made of solid steel bars.

If she was right about Edmund's reasons for sending her here, she knew what to do.

She whistled a single high-pitched note and waited.

For the first time since setting foot in the palace, a genuine smile stretched across her face. She heard it. The unmistakable neighing of her best friend. But she didn't see him.

Etta stepped toward the pen where other horses trotted to and from the door that led to their stalls. Whistling again, she grabbed one of the sun-warmed bars of the fence and hauled herself up to stand on another.

.A substantial chestnut stallion tore past the door and out into the pen, rearing up as he did.

Etta laughed. "Show off."

Vérité skidded to a stop in front of her and nudged her roughly with his nose.

"Mademoiselle," a stable hand called. "I'd stay away if I were you. That one bites."

As if to prove him right, Vérité nipped at her. She smacked his nose, staring into his eyes.

"Thank you, sir," she called back.

The man leaned his shovel against the fence and walked toward her. Vérité stomped his foot.

"Shhhh," she whispered against his neck.

"I ain't seen that horse get close to nobody without sinking his teeth in. He's a mean son of a bitch." He kept his distance from Vérité's back legs.

"Maybe that's because he's not meant to be kept in a cage," she snapped.

"Honey, this ain't no cage. These here animals eat better than I do."

"Maybe it's not a cage, but he isn't free." Just like her.

She slipped from the fence, knowing she'd said too much. She couldn't risk exposure by having them connect Vérité to the thief he was taken from.

She sucked in a breath and rubbed Vérité's nose. Leaning in, she whispered, "I'll be back."

As she walked away, her heart was lighter than before. Vérité was a part of her and it was nice to know that some piece of the girl she was before had remained.

CHAPTER 11

She'd worn the plain clothes his mother gave her instead of the dresses from Camille. Alex noticed it as soon as she appeared at his rooms. He'd sent the captain to get her, a job that was so below him it would have been comical if Anders had any sense of humor.

Etta's golden hair flowed down her back as she peered up at him from the doorway.

"People are going to laugh at me." Was the first thing she said.

"I'll challenge anyone who does," he joked.

She laughed. The first laugh he'd heard from her. "Your reputation precedes you, Your Highness." She walked past him into his suite. "I've heard that there aren't many people you could best in a fight."

"Who speaks such lies?"

"Everyone." She walked toward the sitting room, examining everything as she went. If he didn't know better, he'd think she was memorizing the place to rob him.

He shut the door, allowing them privacy from his guards outside. He'd gotten off on the wrong foot with Etta and it was time to get to know her. When he'd invited her to dine in his rooms, part of him just didn't want to be alone. Before his father was killed, he ate in the hall with the guards, usually with Edmund. With his father gone and Edmund missing, he no longer felt like he belonged with them.

He walked toward the dining area and poured two glasses of wine before stepping beside Etta and handing her one. His eyes widened when he saw what she was flipping through. He'd left his book of sketches out for anyone to see.

"Are these yours?" she asked.

The surprise in her voice niggled at him. "Well ... uh ..." He tugged at his collar and took a sip of wine.

"They're quite good." She flipped the page and stilled as she took in her own face staring back at her.

Alex scratched the back of his neck. "I ... um ... that was after your first fight in the tournament."

She continued to stare at it in silence.

Nervousness was not something Alex was accustomed to experiencing. He tapped his finger against his wine goblet and breathed out heavily.

"I see." She closed the book and looked up at him as she brought her glass to her lips.

Alex's heart thudded against his ribs. She continued to stare. Wishing he could read her mind, he cleared his throat to break the spell and took the sketchbook from her.

"I don't show my drawings to people." He set it on the bookshelf. "I'd appreciate your discretion.

Her lips parted, and a beat passed before she spoke. "You're quite good."

The sudden kindness in her eyes stole the breath from his lungs. In the short time he'd known Etta, she'd been fierce, brave, strong-willed, and even cruel at times... never kind. The minute he began to think he understood her, she proved him wrong.

She blinked, and the coldness returned to her gaze. He'd do anything to see that other girl again. He raised his hand and reached out to tuck a strand of soft golden hair behind her ears, letting his fingers drift down over her cheek.

She held in a breath and the world stopped.

All too soon, Etta jumped back out of his reach. "Any word from Edmund, Your Highness?"

"Please don't call me that." He cleared his throat. "What I mean is that we're going to spend a lot of time together. I want to be friends."

"Friends." She tested the word and a pained look he didn't understand crossed her face. "People are still going to laugh."

"Why do you say that?"

"You're going to be king. I'm just a girl, only eighteen-years-old, and I'm supposed to be your protector."

"Are you saying you want me to release you?"

"No, I'm just preparing you. I've been laughed at for much of my life. No one takes a woman warrior seriously in Gaule. I can handle it. You, on the other hand, are used to ass-kissers."

He suppressed a smile. There was the girl he'd met among the tents before the tournament. It warmed him to think the fights didn't take that away. "The people that matter know what the king's protector really is."

"And what is that?"

"Someone to take an arrow for the king."

She set her glass down and planted her hands on her hips. "So I'm to be your shield? Are you going to cower behind me if we are attacked?"

He drained the last of his wine.

"Make no mistake," she said, stepping forward to within arm's reach. "I am more than a shield. In the tournament, you saw only part of what I can do. I have been training for this my entire life."

That didn't make any sense. They'd only announced the tournament weeks ago.

She realized she'd said something she shouldn't have and tried to back up, but he grabbed her arm, his touch scorching her skin.

"Who are you, Etta?" he asked.

"I am no one."

"Oh, I very much doubt that."

Her mouth parted, but she didn't speak, the spell holding them in place once again.

A throat cleared behind them and Alex ripped his hand from her arm before turning to face his mother.

The Dowager Queen Catrine was clad in an elegant green dress that flowed out from her hips. Her midnight black hair was done up as if she was going to a ball. As always, she played the part of queen well when in the public eye. She hadn't been letting anyone other than her maids into her rooms since the king's death. Her grief surprised Alex because she'd always seemed resentful of his father.

When he'd asked her to go to Etta, he'd been surprised by her eagerness. When she'd suggested this dinner, that surprise turned to wariness.

"Mother." Alex hurried toward her and pulled her into a hug. She wrapped her arms around his back. Of his parents, she'd been the affectionate one.

"My boy." She pulled back to look at him.

Before he could say anything else, she pushed away from him and faced Etta.

"Dear girl, I'm glad you decided to join us."

Etta bowed lower than she'd ever done for Alex or his father. When she rose, she was smiling.

"Mother," Camille said from the doorway. "Don't bother talking to her. She won't be here long."

Alex started to speak, but his mother held up a hand. "Camille, she won your father's tournament. She beat many fully-grown men with years of training in the palace guard. I think she deserves our respect."

Camille huffed, pitching forward as Tyson knocked into her on his way into the room.

"Sorry, Sis." Tyson grinned, throwing a wink to Etta.

"And where have you been?" Alex asked tiredly. "I haven't seen you all week."

Tyson stole a roll from the table and shoved it in his mouth with a shrug.

Alex groaned and rubbed his eyes. When he looked back to Etta, she was watching his family in wonder. What kind of family had she given up to enter the tournament and move to the palace? He didn't know which would have been worse. Giving them up, or not having anything to give up at all.

Etta never had any siblings. She'd been a solitary person and never wished for any, but as she listened to the chatter of Alex's family, she saw what it could be like to have a family.

Her father had been everything she needed. When her mother was alive, she'd given enough love for ten families. But their dinners were never like this. There was no Tyson roaring with laughter. No Alexandre grinning as if no one was watching. Even Camille played her role well, scowling at her brothers.

And just as this morning, Queen Catrine was everything Etta remembered. When she was a girl—before her father allowed her to begin training with a sword—her mother would drag her along to tea with the queen. Their families were close, once upon a time.

Camille never paid her much mind despite being the same age, but Alex ... she stole a glance at him before looking down at the fowl on her plate. Some part of her deep inside wanted to be recognized, to be remembered.

"Children," Catrine said softly, ignoring the fact that none of them were children any longer. She set her fork down and pushed her plate aside, folding her hands on the table. "This is the first time we've all been together since your father's death."

"Whose fault is that, Mother?" Camille asked harshly.

The queen bowed her head in shame. "I am sorry. I have been overcome with grief for ..." she swallowed hard. "The man I loved."

Etta watched her carefully, seeing everything as she'd been taught. The sheen across her brow spoke of nervousness, but the strain around her eyes was proof of her grief. What was she hiding?

The queen went on. "Tomorrow we bury your father and begin a new chapter in this kingdom's history." She smiled at Alex. "Alexandre, my boy, we've been preparing you for this your whole life. It is your birthright. May you do better for our people than your father."

All eyes snapped to her and color rose in her cheeks as her words came back to her.

Camille rose from her chair and threw her napkin on the table, glaring at her mother. "Father was the greatest king Gaule has ever had. Alex couldn't shovel his horse's shit." She stormed from the room.

A stillness descended until her footsteps faded away.

Alex barely breathed.

"Don't worry, Alex," Tyson said. "I'm sure father would have let you shovel his horse's shit."

Alex laughed at the joke but his face was strained.

Catrine smiled and fixed her warm eyes on Etta. "We have an uphill battle to climb, my dear, but you are now a part of this family as my husband's protector was before."

Etta wiped her mouth, the movement hiding her shaking hands. The way the queen was looking at her ... it was as if she knew something.

"Well." Catrine finally tore her eyes away. "We must discuss the ball."

“There’s nothing to discuss,” Alex cut in. “I canceled it.”

“And I uncancelled it.”

A grin spread across Tyson’s face, but Alex shook his head.

“Father just died. The kingdom is still in mourning. We cannot have a ball.”

“Son.” She reached over to cover his hand with hers. “The coronation ball is a tradition—one your father would have wanted us to keep. The people need this.” She tilted her head to the side. “You love balls and now you’re becoming king. However you got there, whatever we’ve been through, that is something to be celebrated and honored.”

Alex nodded, his eyes shining.

“In the weeks after the ball, you must also journey into the village among the people. You’ll spend time with them, speak with them, and show them that our kingdom is still in good hands.” She smiled. “Because it is, my boy.” Her eyes fluttered closed for a brief moment as she breathed deeply. “Oh what a king you will make.”

Alex cleared his throat in embarrassment, flicking his eyes to Etta for a second.

The queen pushed back her chair and stood, straightening her dress. “It's late. Tyson and I will be going."

Tyson shrugged and stood to follow her, leaving Etta alone with Alex once more.

Neither spoke for a moment before Alex leaned back in his chair. "Who are your people, Etta?"

"I don't have people." Since her father's death, it was the truth.

"Everyone has someone." He thought for a moment. "Is it so wrong to want to know the person who is going to stand at my side in the years to come?"

"I'm sorry, your Highness."

"Alex."

"What?"

"Call me Alex when we are alone."

That was a line she refused to cross. He asked for friendship when he did not know the barrier her history created between them. A Basile and a Durand couldn't be friends. Look where it had gotten her father.

"Your Highness," she said sternly, pushing back from the table. "As you so graciously put it before, I’ll be standing in front of you as the dangers come, not at your side." She stood and stepped around her chair. "You say you wish to know me, yet you do not listen. From your seat of privilege, you're incapable of seeing what's truly in front of you. When I say I have no people, I am not lying." She turned her back on him and walked to the door. As her hand grasped the metal knob, she spoke once more. "Everyone I've ever loved is dead."

The moon was high in the night sky by the time Etta made it outside, its silver glow settled over the castle grounds. As a child, she'd loved night within the walls. The stillness was captivating. Candlelight lit the windows of houses as she passed by. She'd spent her younger years thieving, never truly needing the items she stole. It was for the fun of it. So, she knew every alleyway, every low rooftop, every hiding spot.

Her eyes flitted between them as she walked. It took a while to feel comfortable with the fact that she didn't need to hide. She was no longer a child sneaking out of her house.

Each of the guards knew who she was. They'd seen her cut down their comrades in the tournament. As she walked, they kept their distance, but their eyes followed her.

The stables were quiet with the horses in their stalls for the night. A single stable hand sat dozing on a bale of hay near the hanging saddles against the wall.

Horses snorted and stomped their feet as she passed their stalls, looking for her beautiful boy. The white triangle around Vérité's eyes stood out against the dark. She smiled when she saw him and held up a finger as if he'd understand what that meant.

Walking on light feet toward the sleeping hand, she took the lantern that was positioned on the floor by his feet and went back to Vérité.

"Better?" she asked.

Vérité kicked at the door to his stall.

"Hold your horses, would you?" She laughed at her own joke. Vérité didn't seem amused. Clutching the lantern in one hand, she unlatched the door to his stall with the other and then grabbed a fist-full of his light mane to keep him from running off, not like she thought he actually would.

She led him out into the pen and let go. He trotted in a circle around the open space before returning to her. She kissed his nose.

"I'm surrounded by enemies, Vérité." She paused. "But they don't look like enemies." She backed away and hauled herself up to sit on the fence. Vérité moved close once again.

"I thought they'd all be like the king, but it isn't that simple." She cocked her head. "Remember Father? You know, the man you kicked once." She laughed at the memory of her father trying to control Vérité. He was a wild horse. The only way to tame him was to realize he was the one in control.

"Father told me that my head and my heart would disagree sometimes, but that the thinker, rather than the dreamer, begged obedience because only he was not susceptible to pretty fantasies." She scratched the horse's soft nose. "I think father obeyed his heart and the pretty fantasy turned into a vicious nightmare." A long breath whistled past her teeth. "I wish he was here to advise me. I'm so tired. My entire life has been spent in preparation to serve someone I've been bred to hate just on the basis of my name. It would be so much easier if ..."

Before she could finish, Vérité broke away from her and reared up, his neigh breaking the stillness of the night.

Etta whipped around to find Vérité freaking out on a travel-stained blond man.

"Edmund," she whispered, jumping from the fence.

She whistled once and Vérité began to calm. One more whistle and the horse stopped completely and walked back to her to give her shoulder a nudge. She stepped around him to see Edmund standing there with a wild look in his eye.

"Keep that thing away from me."

She laughed. "I don't think Vérité likes you."

"Yeah, well I've heard he doesn't like anyone."

She buried her face in the horse's flank.

"You are a sight for tired eyes." He smiled. "I didn't know you knew how to laugh."

She snorted. "Because there was so much to laugh about as we were hacking our way through the tournament?"

"Wow, you sure know how to make us sound horrible."

"Aren't we horrible?"

"I don't really know." He scratched the back of his neck.

Looking at Edmund, she couldn't believe she'd planned to kill him. It was the rules of the tournament, but his kind eyes would've haunted her for the rest of her life. Instead, here she was, standing in front of someone who seemed very much like a friend.

"How did you get me that note when you've been gone?" she asked, kicking at the ground.

He lifted one shoulder in a shrug. "I left it with the queen, expecting her to get it to you right after I was sent on my mission. Catrine has a soft spot for me." He winked.

Etta rolled her eyes. "Well, I didn't get it until today, but thank you."

"The great warrior, protector of the soon-to-be king is thanking me?"

At the mention of Alex, she grew serious. "He's been worried."

"Alex is always worried about something." He shrugged it away as if it meant nothing.

"Edmund, I don't think he's been sleeping and he barely touched his dinner tonight."

"Are you and he getting on then?" He raised his brow, but something else hid in his tone. Was it jealousy?

"No," she snapped. "But if I am to live here, the least I can do is share a meal with the man. I may not like him, but he's just lost his father and his best friend has been missing."

"Compassion. Not something I'd expect from a trained killer."

"I wasn't trained to kill. I was trained to protect." At the admission, she clamped her teeth down on her lip.

"And what, pray tell, were you trained to protect?"

Her eyes darted around, knowing full well there could be listeners anywhere. Then the world stilled. The sounds of cicadas faded away with the breeze. Vérité's snort of surprise rang loud in the bubble of quiet Edmund created.

"You have many secrets, Etta."

She wanted to tell him everything. The curse. Life in the forest. Her mission. But to do so would reveal her identity as the daughter of the man who killed the king. The kingdom was in mourning because her father was protecting her.

And Edmund was loyal to the crown. So, she began to spin a tale.

"I grew up in the Black Forest." At least that part wasn't a lie even if her earliest years were spent in this very castle. "That's where most of the magic folk who escaped the purge live. They couldn't escape Gaule because once the wards were in place, no one with magic in their blood could cross the border."

"How did no one know you were there?"

She breathed out a long breath, shoring up her lies with bits of truth. "Viktor Basile."

A flash of anger crossed his face. He hated the king's assassin. He took a step away from her and she continued.

"Viktor had wards around the forest to hide us. My father was a friend of his. He trained me to be the protector of the forest."

"Then why enter the tournament?"

"Some things are more important. I wanted to get close to the crown to protect my people on a grander scale."

Edmund rushed at her, pushing her up against the fence.

Vérité reared up and ran the length of the pen in a panic.

Edmund's hand closed around her throat. "Are you here to harm Alex?"

She shook her head, unable to speak.

"Do not lie to me!"

She'd only seen this side of him once, when he'd attacked her in her tent. Head swimming from a lack of oxygen, she brought her arms up in a flash, aiming for his throat. He released her and reeled back, coughing.

He came at her again and she sidestepped him. He grabbed her arm and spun her back to meet him. "It should have been me," he growled. "I should be the one protecting him."

"But you couldn't beat me." She kicked her leg out, catching him in the knee. He released her and threw a jab.

Any normal day, he could probably win in hand to hand combat. Speed was only a match for strength when weapons were involved. But he was exhausted and stumbling from his travels. He'd arrived back from his mission and found her when he was stabling his horse.

She danced out of his reach. "Edmund, stop."

"Alex is the best man I know," he snapped, reached for her again. "I'll kill you before I let you hurt him."

She caught his next punch between both of her hands and twisted his arm as she rammed her shoulder into his stomach. He flipped over her back and landed on the ground, face up. She pinned him there with her knee and scowled down into his red face.

"I'm not going to hurt him." Her curse made sure of that. Hurting Alex meant hurting herself.

Every interaction she'd had with Edmund rolled through her mind. Him risking his life in the tournament. The promise he'd pulled from her before the final fight. He'd been willing to give his life. Not for king and country, but for Alex.

She stumbled off of him, landing hard on her rear. "You're in love with him."

He refused to look at her as he lay on his back, breathing heavily, his eyes raised to the stars above.

"Does he know?" she asked softly, sympathy blooming in her gut.

"Of course not." He rolled onto his side and the light from the lantern lit the fear in his eyes. In the magical community, it wasn't uncommon for one man to love another. The stories said that Bela had been a place where love was celebrated in any form it took. But Gaule was different. Alex's father hanged men for it.

Edmund must have sensed the direction her thoughts took, because he said once again, "Alex is a good man."

"God, I hope so." For the first time in her life, she wanted more than anything for Alex Durand, her enemy by birth, to be a man she didn't have to hate.

CHAPTER 12

Death didn't come like a spirit, quiet in the night. This time it was the bludgeon, pounding into Gaule until there was nothing left but rubble.

The king was dead.

Killed by the most notorious magic man.

It was no wonder that the people were in disarray. There was danger coming. Alex could feel it. With the wards gone, there was a danger he never thought he'd have to face. They'd been protected, and it made La Dame Dracon into a bedtime story, a figure from history. But now she could be just biding her time. Would she come for them?

The sun had barely risen, but Alexandre was preparing. Today he would bury his father. A man who'd kept them safe.

A knock sounded on his door and he finished lacing up his shining black boots before answering it to reveal Edmund. The pressure in his chest eased upon seeing his missing friend.

He stepped back to allow him in and as soon as the door was shut, he pulled him into a hug, pounding a fist on his back.

Edmund chuckled as Alex stepped back uncomfortably.

"Sorry," Alex said. "I'm just... I expected the worst."

"Sorry for the delay."

"When did you get in?"

"Late last night. I was on my way to report to you when I ran into the queen. She said something about you not sleeping much so if I woke you up, I was a dead man."

"Now that you're back, the captain of the guard won't have to follow me around like a puppy. That'll be your job."

"Cute, your Highness." Edmund grimaced. "Just don't let any of your other guards hear you call us puppies. And there are many more senior guards than I to be placed as head of your personal guard. I'm sure my father would rather appoint one of them."

"Your father will listen to his king."

Edmund bowed deeply. "That's right. It'll be hard to get used to you as king."

Alex swatted his head. "Stand up, you idiot." He turned toward his bed to pick up his jacket from where it was draped and a twinge of pain shot through him. He stiffened.

"You okay?" Edmund asked.

"Yeah, it's just strange. I woke up feeling like I'd gone a few rounds in a fight."

Edmund barked out a laugh. "You? Right."

Alex glared. "Come on. My advisers want to meet before the proceedings today and you can report there so you don't have to do it twice."

Edmund and three other guards followed Alex to the council chambers.

Duke Leroy and Duchess Moreau stayed seated when he entered. That would change soon enough.

"Good morning," Alex said stoically. "Well, terrible morning actually. In a couple of hours, we bury my father, but before that, I will be crowned. No large ceremony. Your attendance is required, and it will take place in the chapel."

"Fine, fine." Duke Leroy waved a hand in front of his face.

Duchess Moreau considered him thoughtfully before turning to Edmund. "I see that Edmund has returned. I'm sure his reports will coincide with the ones I have received from the border, but let's hear what he has to say."

Edmund cleared his throat nervously. He could face a man twice his size in a fight to the death, but being involved in the Crown's business made him shifty.

"There's nothing there, sire. We journeyed to the border and tested the wards using the prisoners we'd taken. They were able to cross over despite being of magic stock. The wards are gone."

Nothing he said was a surprise, but it still sucked the air from Alex's lungs.

"What of Dracon?" Duke Leroy asked. "Are they preparing to invade?"

"Not that we could tell. That's what struck us as odd. Our orders were to inspect the wards and return, but we couldn't come back without a glimpse into what was to come. When I said there was nothing there, I didn't only mean the wards. Bela is abandoned."

"Bela has been abandoned for generations, boy." Leroy rolled his eyes dramatically.

Alex growled. "Edmund is the head of the king's personal guard. He will be spoken to as such."

Leroy's expression turned sour, but next to him Duchess Moreau suppressed a grin.

Edmund coughed briefly and continued. "The towns of Bela have been abandoned, yes, but the roads are still used by travelers." He met the prince's intense gaze. "If the wards are gone, why aren't the people in Gaule with magic in their blood running for their lost kingdom? Or any safer kingdom, for that matter."

"There are no more magical folk in Gaule." Leroy leaned back in his chair smugly, crossing his hefty arms over his chest and nodding to Alex. "Your father and I saw to that."

Alex shivered, remembering the days of the purge. His father rode with Duke Leroy on one side and Anders on the other to lead the army against their own people. A necessary evil.

"Don't be an idiot, Leroy," the Duchess said. "Many escaped those awful days and then were trapped by the wards. This young guard's question is a valid one. Why are they staying?"

"Not only that," Edmund went on. "We didn't go as far as the abandoned castle of Bela or any of the towns, but we did go to the border of Dracon and walked along the wall surrounding the kingdom. They don't appear to be mobilizing."

Alex tapped a finger against his chin and contemplated his advisers. "You two would remember La Dame more than I would. I was a child when we broke off our allegiance to her."

The Duchess leaned forward. "She would have known the instant the wards fell. She's been watching us since the day Viktor Basile crafted them. She's dangerous, your Highness. More dangerous than you can imagine. As a child, I had a magic woman for a tutor and she taught me much. Magic is passed down through a family, but it doesn't appear the same way in two people. One person may be able to heal while another controls one of the elements. Some can conjure light. There are many different manifestations. La Dame can mold her magic into whatever form she needs it to take. No one knows how ancient she is, but if you look back on many of the events in history, her side usually came out on top. The tragedy of Bela is probably her biggest achievement. Through subtle moves over many generations, she destroyed an entire kingdom."

Alex paced the length of the room before stopping near her and sitting in the open chair to her left, forgetting decorum for the moment. Teachings of Bela were prohibited from the prince's education, but it was more important than ever that he knew all the facts.

"The only thing my tutors told me of Bela was that it was destroyed by magic," he said. "And that Bela was once our enemy, crushing entire armies with their power."

"Your father was a foolish man then. He probably thought the wards would hold indefinitely so Bela and Dracon would forever be on the outside." She smiled briefly. "Viktor either didn't explain that one's magic dies with them or your father was too blinded to listen."

"Annette," Lord Leroy warned.

Duchess Moreau barely glanced at the duke before continuing. "Bela was once the greatest kingdom of them all. It prospered and flourished." She smiled. "My grandmother told me of her journeys there and the beauty she beheld. Their most celebrated king and queen were Aurora and Phillip Basile."

"Basile? You're telling me the king and queen of legend were Basiles?"

She nodded. "Some people suspected Viktor's line, but the Basiles were said to have the only magic that could match La

Dame. Viktor didn't have the families power. Basile isn't an uncommon name in Bela and no one could be sure. Aurora and Phillip fought against La Dame with everything they had—yes she is even older than that—and it eventually destroyed them. People speak of a curse, but that is just lore. Their eldest son died before he could wear the crown. A kingdom's magic is only as strong as their rulers and this son was the strongest of them all. It is said that in each generation after, the firstborn child was lost. Eventually, the kingdom weakened enough for La Dame to crush them."

"If she's so powerful, why did she have to wait until they were in a weakened state?"

The Duchess met his eyes, the corner of her mouth dropping sadly. "Because, my prince, the only thing that can defeat La Dame is a fully-powered Basile."

"Then we must find the descendants of this Aurora and Phillip."

Duke Leroy shot to his feet, his face going red. "That is enough. We will not be using evil to defeat evil. Magic has no place in Gaule and it never will. What you speak of is blasphemy." He stormed from the room.

Duchess Moreau hadn't moved during his rant, but her shoulders dropped and her focus shifted to her hands. "I am sorry, your Highness. Even if Viktor was a Basile, we don't know where his daughter is. Hidden, no doubt. I'm afraid we are very much on our own."

Alex left the room with Edmund by his side. Today was an important day, but his mind was not on his coronation, or with his father. It was with his people. The border was quiet now, but they were no longer protected. One day soon they would face their greatest fears and La Dame would have no mercy.

CHAPTER 13

The wooden dummy stared with accusing eyes. You shouldn't be here, it said. You don't belong. A curse does not a protector make.

Crossover. Jab. Jab. Lunge. kick. That would teach it. Etta wiped the sweat from her brow as the sun beat down on the top of her head. She should've stopped already. She was dressed for the ceremony and sweat-soaked hair wasn't anyone's idea of acceptable. She ran a hand over her high ponytail. The golden ends brushed against her lower back.

Freedom. Her few last hours. Soon she'd be even more tied to the prince than she already was. The curse would be fulfilled. She was prepared, but it didn't mean she liked it.

She jumped, twisting to the right, and delivered a hard kick to the abdomen of her dummy. There. That was enough. She wiped her face on her sleeve. One of the maids had tried to get her to allow her face to be painted. Ha. That'd be a mess now.

Looking across the practice yard, her eyes caught movement beneath the archway. Camille stood beside Anders. She leaned close, but not in an intimate kind of way. It was more of an "I'm up to something" way. They both glanced toward Etta, matching scowls on their faces. Did Alex know his sister was obviously planning something with the captain? Probably not.

But it wasn't her business. Etta was there for a singular purpose. It wouldn't suit her to get involved in court business. She was here to protect the king's body. That was it.

Etta started walking, her eyes still on them. She rammed into something and stumbled back. Looking up, she came face to face a grim Tyson. In that moment, he looked every bit his fifteen-years.

"Etta," he said, his voice thick. "I didn't see you."

"It's okay, your Highness."

He let out a long breath.

She waited for a moment, remembering her promise from a moment ago to stay out of court business, but then Tyson's eyes began to swim.

"Are you okay?"

"Fine." He wiped angrily at a tear.

"No, you're not." She glanced around, knowing the prince wouldn't want the nearby guards to see him in such a state. She grabbed his arm. "Come on."

He didn't protest as she led him from the palace and out to the outer castle grounds. His eyes stayed focused on his feet as he attempted to hide his face.

They reached the stables. A few horses were in the pen for their morning exercise. Vérité's head snapped up as she approached the fence.

To the stable hand nearby, she said, "Leave. Now."

He took a look at the prince behind her and obeyed.

"Why are we here?" Tyson asked.

She spun to look at him. "Look, I don't know you, but I do know the sadness in your eyes." She didn't say it, but it matched the sadness in her heart for her own father.

He nodded and looked away.

"Do you ride much?" she asked.

"Of course. Every time I go into town."

"Ah, but do you ever just spend time around horses? Talk to them?"

"Talk to a beast?"

"There's no better listener. Want to know a secret?"

He nodded, and she leaned closer.

"I think horses have magic."

"I hope not. My family would probably kill them." He clenched his teeth in disapproval and Etta cocked her head, surprise rushing through her.

The littlest Durand didn't approve of the purge. Interesting. She filed that away for later use and climbed over the fence into the pen. "Come on."

Vérité was at her side as soon as she dropped to the dirt. She reached out to pet his nose, and he nipped at her fingers.

Tyson had been around horses all his life, but Etta wondered what he actually knew about them. She liked to believe she could sense what was in Vérité's heart.

"Careful," she warned. "Vérité here doesn't like strangers."

The most trusting of the Durands, he didn't ask how she already knew the horse. In fact, he didn't ask any questions at all. He moved cautiously toward Vérité. The horse snorted but remained still as Etta rubbed his neck with gentle, soothing strokes.

Tyson's fingers ran along his back and Vérité seemed to shiver in pleasure.

Etta laughed. "I think he likes you, and he doesn't like anyone."

Tyson pulled his hand back and leaned against the fence. The lines around his mouth relaxed, but he squeezed his eyes shut. Another tear escaped his left eyelid and his entire body shuddered.

"Thank you, Etta," he said. "For bringing me here. You aren't as unfeeling as you try to seem."

He hadn't meant it as an insult, but Etta deserved the ill feeling it gave her. Her emotions had been so twisted up since setting foot past the castle gates that she hadn't been able to show anything of herself. If she allowed the Durands to see her as a friend, allowed them to care, what kind of person did that make her? They didn't know her family and how they were supposed to be at odds.

"And I guess you aren't quite as cheery as you attempt to portray." She pointed a finger at his down-turned mouth.

"Do you want to know something awful?"

Etta only responded by pressing her lips together.

"I didn't know my father. Not really. He never had much time for his youngest child. In Alex, he got an heir. In Camille, he got a daughter who worshipped him. But me ... I was only a nuisance. Yet, I seem to be the only one who cares that we will bury him today."

"Your brother has a lot on his mind."

"I know that." He met her eyes. "But he was our father." His head swung from left to right slowly. "And that's not the worst of it."

Etta raised an eyebrow.

"I've always wanted to love him. I don't think I have to know him to love him." Another tear fell. "But he did so much wrong. I just can't. "

Etta's heart ached for the young prince. She leaned against the fence next to him. Vérité, sensing something was amiss, bumped his long nose against the side of Tyson's head. The horse approved of the youth and Etta was beginning to agree. Maybe Tyson was the best of them all.

Tyson rubbed Vérité's neck absently. "I hope my brother is a different kind of king."

"Me too, your Highness."

"I've just spilled my guts to you, Etta. Call me Tyson."

She smiled, her mind still back on what he'd said before. The truth was she didn't know who exactly Alexandre Durand was. Except that in an hour's time, he would be king.

The chapel hummed with anticipation. It hadn't been decorated and the only guests in attendance were the king's advisers, family, and guards. A priest stood at the altar, waiting. This was not a celebration. This coronation wasn't supposed to take place for another ten or twenty years. When a king reached his later years, he planned a coronation for his son as a lavish affair with feasts and tournaments. Now they were hidden away.

Etta stood as the prince walked down the narrow aisle. He wore a perfectly pressed jacket and trousers. A Durand family crest—three intertwining trees with a sword through the middle—was emblazoned on the jacket's arm. Ironic considering Etta's power.

His hair was neatly tied back and shining, and his eyes held a strength she hadn't yet seen. He looked like a king. Etta held her breath until he reached the front and knelt.

She released it in one long puff of air as that invisible thread binding her to Alex tightened. She barely heard anything the priest said and before she knew it, a crown was placed on Alexandre's head and her name was being called.

Her feet moved of their own accord until she was by the new king's side. He'd risen and now watched her expectantly. Her knees bent and hit the stone hard but the pain barely registered. This moment was what her entire life had been about. For she was Persinette Basile, and she was cursed. Her life was not her own. It belonged to the man who now stood in front of her with a golden crown atop his head.

The curse tugged at her, begging to break free. It wanted this. It wanted her pledge, her promise. Magic was a living thing and La Dame's magic lived inside her, tying her to Alex. She looked up at him. Her childhood friend. Her captor. Her enemy. Her king. He was everything and nothing. Important and inconsequential. One day, when her story was told to a future cursed generation, they'd learn of the enemy who was no enemy. The conflicted one. The good one. Everyone told her he was a good man, and now she saw it. His eyes told the full tale.

He smiled in reassurance. Comfort.

She'd been fighting against the hate clawing at her heart, and now she'd won.

So, she lowered her head and touched her forehead to the ground in the greatest sign of respect. She'd killed to be here. Her soul was in tatters. But maybe something good would come from the darkness.

Alex cleared his throat. "I am here to honor my father's last wish. The winner of his tournament is to serve by my side. Etta."

She raised her head to look at him.

"Do you vow to protect the king, to remain at his side, to be a loyal and trustworthy steward of Gaule?"

"I do," she said.

"Do you promise to be honorable and honest."

"Yes."

"Are you prepared to do what is necessary?"

"I am."

"Then rise, Etta, and stand at my side." He extended a hand down to her. "Always."

As she took his hand, the world around her shifted. Energy flowed through their connection as the curse held them together. His eyes swirled as they connected with hers and held fast. Their skin tingled where it met, but neither let go until the power began to subside. As quickly as it rose in them, it was gone.

Something she hadn't known was broken inside her slid into place as if her world was now as it should be. She'd been prepared for pain, for torment. She'd watched her father live with the curse for years. What he hadn't prepared her for was… joy. Completeness. The curse didn't feel like magic, but rather the most natural thing in the world.

Alex's wide eyes held hers for a moment longer, before he dropped her hand, breathing heavily.

She missed his touch instantly. Raising a hand, she trailed her fingertips down his arm. He sucked in a breath.

"What is this?" he whispered.

The truth was on the tip of her tongue, but uttering it would have wide-reaching consequences. She lowered her hand. "I don't know."

He shook himself out of the daze, his eyes never leaving her.

"Alexandre," his mother urged.

He marched down the aisle, throwing one final look back over his shoulder. Etta followed, shifting her eyes to her feet.

How much would Alex question? Would he make dangerous guesses? His father hadn't known the extent of Viktor's curse despite spending years in his company. Etta could keep it hidden as well. She didn't know any of the answers to her million questions. All she knew was that she wanted to feel it again.

Taking note of the crown he wore, people in the palace halls bowed low as Alex passed by. He hurried toward the great hall but Etta knew he only wanted all of this ceremony to end.

Queen Catrine, Camille, and Tyson followed them and their guards with the rest of the nobles bringing up the rear. People were waiting in the hall when they arrived. A platform had been erected in the front of the room and the king's preserved body lay out for all to see. Alex's steps slowed as he neared his father.

Etta looked down on the man, remembering the threats he'd spoken to her. Those threats got him killed. Her father wouldn't have sacrificed his life for any other reason than to save hers.

The dead king's face morphed into that of her father's. Had anyone buried him? Of course, Pierre and Maiya would have seen to it. She'd have to find a way to visit Maiya to ask where he was laid to rest.

Alex shook his head sadly. "I could use your advice, Father."

Etta glanced at Tyson who was slow to hide a look of disgust. His eyes were red, but she now knew it wasn't because his father was dead. It was because he couldn't bring himself to love the dead man and the guilt gnawed at him.

Camille blubbered behind them, but Queen Catrine was eerily calm, almost uncaring, as she stared at her husband. They took their seats, and the priest began to speak, but Etta's mind was once again in a far-off place.

The man on that platform had at one time been as much as a brother to her father. She remembered her days as a child of the court, trying to tag along after her father. The king had no patience for children. She touched her cheek where all those years ago he'd struck her.

And Alex had come to her defense, striking out at his own father. He'd received a beating for that. It was hard to imagine that boy as the same man who believed in the things his father did as king.

Their arms brushed and her chest tightened. This curse was going to be the death of her. But nothing had ever felt so good.

Alex was looking forward to a steaming bath and a soft bed. A funeral and a coronation in the same day took a lot out of him, but he was king now. He didn't get to be tired. He kept his shoulders from sagging as he made his way down the long corridor. Show no weakness and you will have none. It was a lesson from his father.

Etta was silent beside him. She hadn't left his side all day, and it surprised him what a comfort that was. It wasn't the protection aspect; it was just her.

He didn't know what had passed between them during that ceremony, but he wanted more than anything to feel that way again. He'd never been so connected to someone than he had in that moment. His skin hummed with remnants of the energy. Had he imagined it? Was Etta questioning it as well?

He watched her walk with soft, purposeful steps, her silky hair bouncing with each movement. She was the only woman he knew who preferred pants to skirts and embroidered sleeves, but the style suited her. She looked fierce, deadly, his weapon waiting to be unleashed.

Her finger tapping against her leg was the only sign she was nervous.

"Etta?" he asked.

"Your Majesty?" she answered.

He ignored her formality, shaking off the odd sense of it. As much as he was anticipating sleep, he wasn't ready for her to leave him.

"There are things about Gaule you must now learn as protector."

"Tonight?" She narrowed her eyes.

"There may be trouble coming. Follow me, I'll explain." Not wanting to discuss Bela and La Dame where other ears could hear them, he turned in the direction of his rooms. He'd kept his prince's quarters which consisted of a suite of rooms for various purposes- sleeping, eating, bathing, meetings.

When they were inside with the door shut, he lit a lantern and set it on the table before turning to her. She unstrapped her knife sheath and set it aside, offering him a smile.

Something was different about her. Was it the ceremony? He ran a hand over his face. He didn't understand anything. What was happening to him? He was the king and now he had no words to give his protector.

His gut clenched as something fluttered inside it. His cool mask dropped and the heat in his eyes shone through.

Etta bit her lip. "What's going on here?"

He stalked toward her. She retreated up until her back hit the door.

"I don't know," he breathed, his face inches from hers. "All I know is that from the moment I met you, I knew you were special. But today ... do you feel it?"

She nodded, swallowing hard. "Sometimes it's the only thing I feel."

He closed the distance in an instant, claiming her mouth with his. She opened for him, hot and eager. He closed his hands around her wrists and slammed them to the door above her head before sliding his palms down the lengths of them.

She brought her hands down around his neck and he pressed closer, unable to stop himself. An invisible force held him in place as he gripped her hips and kissed her harder. Her fingers tugged at his hair.

"Alex." Her voice cracked against his lips.

He spun her around and pinned her roughly against a bookshelf, knocking a few books to the ground.

They didn't notice. Nothing mattered but them. Nothing existed, save for that moment, that tie binding them together. Their chests rose and fell as one, perfectly in sync.

Then the spell broke, shattering the perfect moment at their feet. Etta pushed Alex away from her, her eyes wild.

She heaved in a few breaths, shaking her head, before rasping, "I'm your protector."

"That doesn't mean anything." He reached for her again and she stepped away. "I told you, it's symbolic."

She shook her head again.

"Etta," he pleaded. "I ..."

"You don't get it." She pointed a finger from herself to him. "This isn't real."

He shook his head in confusion. "Nothing has ever felt more real."

A tear leaked from the corner of her eye. "I'm your protector now. And the first thing I must protect you from is me."

He stepped toward her and gripped her shoulders to force her to stand still and look at him. "When I kissed you, this entire hellish day vanished. The pull you've had on me since that first day of the tournament it's like... magic."

"In your kingdom, Your Majesty, magic only leads to death."

He released her abruptly, and she bowed formally.

"Sleep well, sire. Morning always brings with it new clarity."

She left, and he sank into a chair next to the bookcase. As he dropped his head into his hands, a rush of emotions from the day threatened to push him under their currents.

He yanked the crown from his hair and threw it with a yell. It clattered to the floor and rolled to a stop.

In your kingdom, magic only leads to death.

Her words were true. Is that what he'd felt between them? Magic? But how was that possible?

His father rid the kingdom of magic during the purge. He closed his eyes as the image he'd never forgotten flashed across his mind. He'd always associate the purge with his friend Persinette and her dead mother on the night it all began.

CHAPTER 14

The last time Etta attended a ball was for the queen's birthday. She'd been ten-years-old and was only invited because Queen Catrine had a fondness for the children of the court. Normally, they were kept away.

No children would be present tonight, but every noble of the kingdom would go out of their way, some traveling for days, to be there when their new king gave his first toast. There was to be no more mourning for dead kings. It was Alexandre's wish. If the realm was to withstand the challenges to come, they must look to the future, not the past.

That future had Etta wearing a gown that was much too tight, and rouge that made her look like someone else. She ran her hands down the soft fabric of her pink dress. It hugged every curve before flaring out at the waist. The neckline dipped low into the cleavage of her breasts, leaving her favorite place to stash her knife unavailable.

She lifted the hem of her skirt and strapped a sheath to her thigh. There. Now she didn't feel so naked.

She wished she could wear her sword, but even the protector wasn't allowed a weapon tonight.

She didn't understand how they expected her to protect the king in such a silly frock. And she wouldn't be able to run in the horrid shoes they forced on her. Not like she could breathe enough for that, anyway.

She left her room behind and made her way next door. One of the guards knocked for her.

The face that greeted her wasn't the king's. Camille sneered from the doorway, her eyes narrowing like a predator finding its prey.

"You shouldn't be here," the princess said after a beat of suffocating silence.

"I should be anywhere the king is." Etta cocked her head to the side. "Tell me, how is Anders?"

Shock registered on Camille's face just long enough for Etta to realize she wasn't wrong. They were up to something.

"I won't even pretend to understand what you're talking about." She lowered her voice. "Commoner."

"Camille," Alex snapped, appearing behind her. "I'll never understand why you always have to be a bitch."

Camille reeled back and turned her scowl on Alex. "Watch it, Brother."

"Or what? Father is no longer here to praise your cruelty. I am king and you will treat me as such. Etta is my protector. She will be shown respect."

Camille huffed and stalked back into the room. Alex's eyes met Etta's and flashes of the night before appeared before her eyes.

Don't you feel it?

Sometimes it's the only thing I feel.

She shook her head and bowed. "Your Majesty."

"Etta." He swallowed hard, his eyes roaming from the tops of her breasts pushing against the dress down her long torso and toned, bare arms.

She crossed her arms over her chest to cover herself. "I didn't have a choice in dress."

"It's uh..." He pushed a hand through his hair, knocking his crown off kilter. "You're perfect... I mean, it's perfect."

He startled when Edmund stepped up behind her, still in the doorway. A laugh rumbled through his broad chest. "I can't remember the last time I saw Alex flustered." He pressed a light kiss to Etta's cheek. "I think he's trying to say you look ravishing."

Alex shot him a forbidding look.

"My king." Edmund was still grinning when he inclined his head. "Are we ready to depart?"

"Let's get this over with."

The royal family lined up to walk to the hall together—the dowager queen, the king, the prince and princess. Etta was a step behind them. Edmund and the other guards formed a protective barrier.

The large double doors to the hall stood open and as they entered, the room fell silent. It was packed with people in their finery and every one of them bowed immediately. Gaule was a realm that thrived on structure and tradition.

Alex's voice boomed out. "Rise." He gestured to the string quartet to resume playing and nodded to people on his way to the high table. Queen Catrine took her place to the king's left and Camille moved for the seat on the right. Alex held out a hand to stop her. "That seat belongs to the protector."

A low growl sounded in Camille's throat. Her father used to let her sit in the honored place next to the king. She moved to the other side of her mother. Etta walked to the chair and Tyson nabbed the seat beside her.

She was officially entrenched in the Durand family.

Sweat slickened her palms as she scanned the gathering of Gauleans. These were the very ones who hunted magic folk. As they clustered together, were they conspiring against her people? Were their hearts so filled with fear and hate?

She studied each exit, making note of where the guards stood. It would take her less time to reach the doors than it'd take for them to realize what was happening and draw their weapons.

She shook her head. She wasn't a prisoner, as much as she felt like one surrounded by the nobles of Gaule. But these weren't the people, not truly. They were the ruling class. The armies might have carried out massacres and mass arrests during the purge, but they had orders. A breath shuddered out of her and she gave a weak smile to the man who leaned over to fill her wine glass.

With shaking fingers, she grasped the stem of the glass and brought it to her lips, in need of some liquid calming.

The first course came, but the food was too rich for her sour stomach. Alex barely spoke to her as the night wore on and more food was set in front of them. He looked like he wanted to be there even less than Etta did.

As the final dishes were whisked away, a hushed silence fell over the gathering and expectant eyes turned on the king. This was what they'd been waiting for; why they'd traveled so far. Their king was about to give his first speech.

Alex stood, clasping his hands in front of his chest. "Lords and Ladies of Gaule, I am honored by your presence." His voice held a depth she hadn't heard before. "My reign has begun during a trying time. My father, may he rest in peace, kept this kingdom safe for many years."

Etta stared down at the table so her rolling eyes couldn't be seen. Her father was the one who'd provided that protection.

Alex continued. "Darkness is coming. There is no stopping it this time. We have no wards and the ones who will come for us are armed with a far greater power than we could hope to have. It's going to take the entire realm working together. We must root out this pestilence. We must defend our land from dark magic."

A cheer rose up from the crowd and Etta's knuckles turned white as she gripped the table. They didn't hear what she did. Dark magic. Not magic. She watched him, this conflicted king.

"We must kill the magic folk," someone yelled. Others voiced their agreement.

Alex's face paled as more people spoke up and he lost control to his blood thirsty nobles. Gaule was more far gone than anyone thought and Alex was at the mercy of their desires.

"We must be careful," he said. "Prepared. We do not want to repeat the horrors of the purge."

"Why not?" a rotund man with graying hair said. "The purge was a great event in our history. You would do well, sire, to be more like your father."

Alex reached for his wine goblet and raised it up. "To Gaule." He drained it and set it heavily on the table as those in attendance followed suit.

Collapsing back into his chair, he ran a hand over his face.

"Don't let them beat you down, My king." A man led two rosy-cheeked girls toward the high table. "We all know you will carry on your father's legacy and rulings. Your father was good at acting unaffected. You'd do well to practice that skill."

Alex sat up straighter. "Lord Leroy," he said. "It is a pleasure."

"That's better." Lord Leroy nodded.

Alex pasted his usual charm across his face and looked to the girls with a wink. "Ladies, you both look like rare gems tonight." One of the girls giggled, but the other only stared at the ground.

"That's Alex's betrothed," Tyson said, leaning toward Etta to whisper. He pointed to the girl studying the ground. "Amalie."

"Is she always so ..." She didn't need to finish.

"When she's around my brother. She's scared of him. She's only fifteen, my age. They won't be married for years yet, but my father and Leroy tied them to each other when she was a child."

"You sound fond of her."

He thought for a moment. "She's kind–unlike the rest of her family. Her older sister, Liza is a friend of Camille's. She's married to a lord up North who is too old to travel to things like this. It was a cruel match, but it brought the Leroys a lot of money. She travels on his behalf and beds half the nobles while she's at it."

Etta let out a laugh, getting the attention of Lord Leroy and his daughters.

"Have I introduced you to my protector?" Alex asked.

Amalie raised her gray eyes to Etta's and smiled softly. She had pale skin and a light dusting of freckles that created a delicate beauty. Etta was entranced. But if this girl was to be queen, she too would be an enemy of the Basiles.

"Hello." Her voice held a musical lilt. Etta glanced sideways at Tyson who seemed to be under some sort of spell.

Liza grunted out a greeting.

Lord Leroy said nothing to her before turning back to the king. "Why don't you and Amalie enjoy yourselves, sire. The dancing has begun."

As if the speech and response were already forgotten, Alex stood and walked around the table before offering his betrothed his hand and leading her away. Her family followed them.

Etta was still watching them when Edmund stepped up to the table and ushered an exaggerated bow. "My lady, would you care to take pity on a poor guard and dance with him?"

Etta grinned. "I don't know. I quite like my feet and don't enjoy the thought of being trod over."

He feigned insult and placed a hand over his heart. "I promise you will return with your feet intact."

"In that case." She let him guide her to the dance floor and take her into his arms.

He hadn't been lying. As soon as he began to move, she knew he was as skilled on the dance floor as he was in the fighting arena. He moved with an impressive combination of power and grace.

The music sped up and exhilaration rushed through her as they glided through the steps. Her father spent many hours teaching her the court dances. He'd done everything to prepare her for life in service to the crown.

"I would have rescued you from your table sooner." Edmund grinned. "But I got sidetracked. I didn't want you to have to endure the boorish company of the king any longer than necessary." He laughed and she realized the king and Amalie were next to them, moving in sync. Edmund glanced over her shoulder. "Oops, I'm afraid the king heard me."

"You're terrible." Etta laughed.

"And you're having a good time." He spun her so they were out of hearing range from the king. "But seriously, he's too worried. He loves these things. You know his reputation. It's well-earned. He's the smiling prince turned dour king. I'm worried about him."

"Edmund, I admire how much you care. But he's king now. He was bound to change. The weight of the kingdom rests on his shoulders."

"The nobles don't take him seriously yet. That's his own fault, of course. He preferred parties and women to meetings at his father's side. He'd rather have been sitting atop the walls with his sketches than in the practice yard. He was always seen as the joke. Even among the guards. He was supposed to have grown up and been more settled by the time he had to rule them."

"We don't choose our fates. It isn't for us to decide when our destiny is upon us."

"Then there's the problem of having a beautiful woman following you around." He winked. "But then, he's royalty. He's always been surrounded by alluring women. But the way he looks at you..." There was no pain in his voice. Edmund knew he was in love with a man he could never have, but all he wanted was the best for Alex.

Etta had never met a more honorable man. She took her hand from his and squeezed his shoulder. "He's lucky to have you."

"And you, Protector, are either going to be his salvation or his destruction." He flicked his eyes toward Alex. "I'm going to go save both him and Amalie. Neither of them want to be forced together."

He led them over and bowed slightly. "My king, may I dance with your betrothed?"

"That's not up to me," Alex said.

Edmund turned to Amalie who gave him a grateful smile and placed her hand in his.

They left Alex and Etta standing in the middle of the dance floor. Alex cleared his throat. "Would you like to dance?"

"I'm not sure that's a good idea."

He leaned in. "And why not? Afraid to be seen having a good time? It might make people fear you a bit less, and we couldn't have that." He chuckled.

"You find yourself quite humorous, don't you?" she asked.

He grinned and slid his hands around her waist to draw her in. "Humorous, no. Charming, absolutely."

"Hmmm," she said, allowing him to take her hand.

"No more excuses," he whispered, pulling her closer. "I've been wanting to dance with you since you appeared at my door."

A blush crept up her neck and her feet began to move.

Etta slid her free hand around his back, feeling his muscles bunch beneath his jacket.

He spun her across the dance floor as if they were the only two present. Her heart beat frantically and she wanted to be closer, so much closer. But she couldn't. It took everything she had not to get lost in his touch.

Movement at the corner of the ballroom snapped her back to reality.

He slowed his dancing and caught sight of his sister and Anders conspiring in the shadows. There was no surprise in his eyes. "Camille has Anders using his men to search for magic folk inside Gaule."

"Aren't his men also yours?"

"Yes." He snapped his eyes to her. "I've known about their arrangement since my father died. I know everything that goes on in this palace."

A shiver raced through her. There were some things he didn't know.

"Camille doesn't trust me to deal with the problem. If she wasn't family, she'd probably be in the dungeon." He ran a tired hand over his jaw. "I need to find her a noble to marry and remove her from the castle, but she's my sister. I don't want to banish her."

Etta touched his arm. "You have to weigh the harm she'll cause against your love for her." She hesitated. "The line between being a good man and a foolish one is drawn in sand. Easily erasable. Always movable. Never where you expect it to be."

"Did you just call your king a foolish man?" One corner of his mouth curved up. "I could have you punished for that."

"Then who would protect your dim-witted ass?"

His smile grew, and she matched it.

Looking toward the highborn ladies waiting along the wall, Etta shook her head. "There are others you should be dancing with."

He followed her line of sight and she didn't miss his grimace.

She hid her smile as she released him and stepped back. "Would it be okay for the protector to retire for the evening?"

"Yes, but you will leave behind a jealous king who most likely won't be seeing his bed for some time yet."

Etta laughed and inclined her head. "Have fun, your Majesty."

CHAPTER 15

After his first few weeks as King, Alex had accomplished nothing more than putting out fires among the nobles. Money had to be raised to repair the damage from the quakes. People flocked to the castle to regale the king with tales of those intimidating them with magic. It seemed the villages had a problem, but the rural areas suffered worse.

There were more magic folk still living in Gaule than he'd realized. Part of him was pleased that the purge wasn't a complete success. He'd never advocate murder. But a greater part of him recognized the danger they now faced.

It was to be his first trip into town since his father died. The first with a crown nestled in his inky hair.

Sleep had eluded him much of the night. When it did come, it was interrupted by images that left him gasping and clawing at the bed. He leaned against the fence where horses watched him curiously.

Memories flashed before him and he was twelve again.

"Father," he'd asked. "Why are you doing this?" He struggled to keep up with his father's long strides.

The king stopped when he reached his waiting horse, held in place by an older stable hand. He stepped into the stirrup and vaulted up into the saddle.

"Father." Tears ran down the young prince's face. "They're gone. Viktor. Persinette."

The king's eyes cut through his son. "Don't worry, boy. We won't let them get far. We will rid this land of magic once and for all."

He kicked his horse and thundered past the gates with a stream of soldiers following.

Alex fell to his knees. Magic was evil, but his friend wasn't. Persinette and her father were on their side. He was sure of it. He called after his father, but he was long gone.

That night, and many that followed, saw blood run through the streets of Gaule. There'd been no turning back. He was bred to distrust the power he didn't understand, bred to obey and worship his father. So much so, that now he didn't know who to trust. He didn't know how to protect his kingdom.

"Sire," Edmund's voice broke through the haze in his mind. "The horses are ready."

Alex regarded him, clapping a hand on his shoulder. "Thank you, Edmund."

Etta led her horse from the stables. She'd chosen one no one else would have. The beast was wild and angry, much like her. Alex sighed. She hadn't spoken more than a few polite words to him all morning. Neither had acknowledged the closeness they felt since their kiss. Dancing with her the night before was the only time during the ball that he didn't want to throw his crown across the room and make a mad dash for the border.

It was one of the many things Alex no longer understood.

Why was he so drawn to her?

She was difficult and rude. She had an obvious disdain for his father. Nothing about her was simple. Her features were strong and hardened, instead of the delicate faces he'd experienced among the women at court.

He shook his head and climbed onto his shining black steed. His bow—his weapon of choice—was tied to the saddle.

Etta snorted when she saw it.

"Is there a problem?" Alex snapped.

"No, your Majesty." She suppressed a grin as she checked the ties on her horse's saddle. "It's just that I didn't know we were going hunting."

"I suppose I don't want to know what you're talking about, but curiosity has gotten the better of me. Explain."

Edmund walked his horse up beside the two. "I think she means that if you want to protect yourself, a bow is as useful as a knife when eating soup."

Etta laughed and Alex's irritation subsided as he lost himself in the sound.

"Edmund." Etta looked sideways. "Maybe you should help his majesty with his sword-skill."

"Me? Why not you? You're the protector." He feigned indignation and hauled himself onto his horse.

"Because if I were to harm the king, my daddy couldn't get me out of the dungeon." Her horse snorted as she pulled herself onto him and swung her leg over.

He held a hand to his heart. "That was a low blow, lady Etta."

"I'm no lady."

Before either of them could respond, she kicked her horse, and they started down the path.

People crammed themselves along the sides of the streets to get a look at their newly crowned king. There were cheers and excitement. All nerves drifted far away as Alexandre Durand took in his people. They'd come for him. Only him. Not his father. He couldn't remember ever seeing this kind of reaction for his father. It was so very different from the reception he'd received from his nobles.

He sat up straighter in his saddle and lifted his arm in a wave.

Edmund snorted beside him. "You're enjoying this."

Alex shot him a grin. "After the public flogging I received at the ball, why shouldn't I?" He glanced back to where Etta sat perfectly atop a horse that no one else had dared to ride.

She caught his eye as he laughed. "Is there a problem, your Majesty?"

"I can't believe you haven't been thrown from your horse yet."

She drew her lips to the side. "Is that a challenge?"

"I would never issue you a challenge you couldn't win."

Etta smirked and bent forward to whisper to her horse. Her legs squeezed in tighter and she jerked the reins. The damn horse began to prance as if they'd been practicing the move their whole lives.

The crowd let out a roar of approval, egging Vérité on. He went on for a few moments before returning to his stance and continuing on with the guard's horses.

Alex threw his head back in laughter. Etta didn't look at him. Her eyes shifted toward the people, but her lips twisted as she tried to hide a smile.

The bright sun beat down on them as they came to a stop in the center of town. The market was teeming with villagers who'd followed them through the streets.

Alex slid down from his horse gracefully and his guard did the same. As he watched the people surround him, he breathed out heavily. How was he to lead these people when he didn't know how to keep them safe? Today he'd make the announcement that could change their fates, the fate of the kingdom of Gaule. Today, he'd tell them that their worst nightmare was here. That they were vulnerable.

Those cheers would turn to gasps, the joy to fear. They were about to break.

He clenched his palm tight, fingernails digging into skin, and looked to Etta. She'd been right. Morning always brings clarity. She was meant to see this through with him. Her eyes lifted to his and that same electricity from that night in his room flowed between them. She nodded once, and he knew he could do it.

He was ready to be king.

"The king has an announcement to make," Edmund's voice rose above the rabble and the crowd quieted.

Etta glanced around for a familiar face. A few in this town could point to her as the thief with magic. Then there were the two who could put her mind at ease about her father. But Maiya and Pierre were nowhere to be found.

Alex stepped onto a platform and she followed, scanning for possible dangers.

He cleared his throat. "Hi." He coughed as words failed him.

Uncertainty marred his features, and she stepped closer and dropped her voice. "Honesty, your Majesty. That's what they deserve."

He swallowed and began again. "Our period of mourning for my father has ended. It must. As a kingdom, we must move on to the dangers we face. I am no longer your prince." One of the guards handed up Alex's crown, and he placed it on his head. "I am now Alexandre Durand, forty-second king of the great kingdom of Gaule. And I am here to tell you of the dangers we face. The wards have been destroyed."

A cry rose up from the crowd as panic set in.

"Hear me now—" But before he could continue, a burst of wind blew through the market, stronger than any natural force.

Etta yanked Alex down off the platform.

"What's going on?" he yelled over the deafening noise.

"Magic." She wasn't sure he heard her, and it was probably better if he didn't. She could feel the magic in the air, swirling down upon them. She scanned the rooftops for the source of the wind and found a stocky man with bright red hair. His arms were raised as he called his magic.

More screams rose up as fires erupted out of nowhere. There was no doubt in her mind. Gaule was under attack.

She kept hold of Alex's arm to keep from being separated. Edmund took his place on the other side of the king. "We need to get him somewhere safe."

Edmund was right. They had to get out of there.

"Come on." She patted Vérité's side, and he turned to follow them. They ran into an alleyway and the sounds from the market square faded.

The rest of the king's guards were lost in the mess behind them.

They reached the end of the alley and jogged up the street until they arrived at a familiar shop. Etta yanked on the door but it was locked.

"Maiya," she yelled, pounding her fists against the solid wood. It was cracked, probably from the quake after her father's death. The wood groaned beneath her steady drumming. "Pierre." Sounds came from the alleys nearby and her fists slowed. "Please. Let us in."

As she stopped and turned back to look at the king, considering their next move, the door swung open.

"P-Etta," Maiya cried, flinging her arms around her friend.

"Maiya, we need to come in."

She stepped back and finally noticed Etta's companions. "Of course. Come in. Come in." They rushed inside, shut the door, and latched it.

Maiya dipped into a curtsy. "Your Majesty."

"We owe you a debt," Alex said as he tried to even his breathing.

Etta grabbed Maiya's arm. "I need to talk to you."

She nodded and led Etta to the back room. Alex tried to follow, but the door shut in his face.

As soon as they were alone, Etta's shoulders sagged, and she leaned against the wall, running a hand through her hair.

"I knew it was coming," Maiya confessed suddenly. "The attack. There's a group of magic folk who've been planning it since the wards came down."

"Why didn't you warn me?"

"How was I supposed to do that?" Etta had never seen Maiya look so angry. "I haven't heard a word from you until today. We didn't know if you were dead or if your magic had been found out and you were rotting in their prison." A sob escaped her. "Things have been bad here, Etta. So much of the town was destroyed in the quake. It's not safe to roam the streets."

"Then why don't you pack up and move to the forest?"

"You forget, the forest is no longer protected; the people no longer hidden. They wait for the day they're found and rounded up by the very king you bring to my house tonight."

Etta hesitated. "I don't think Alex is the man his father was."

"But what if he is? This curse will be the death of you."

Etta stepped forward and gripped Maiya's shoulders, craning her neck to look down into her eyes. "I won't let it."

"Will you let it be the death of our people?"

She sucked in a breath. "Of course not. But our people are not saved by launching attacks that only brew anger."

"Then how are our people saved?" Maiya asked.

"I don't know."

"That's ... reassuring."

A tired laugh burst out of her and she pulled Maiya in for a hug. "I missed you." They stood that way for a few moments before Etta pulled back to ask the question that had been tearing at her. "My father ..."

"We buried him in the Black Forest where he would've wanted." She paused. "By the most enchanting stretch of wildflowers. It's strange. I don't recall seeing those anywhere else in that forest." She gave Etta a knowing look.

A weight lifted from her heart. Her father was home. Better yet, he was in her sanctuary. She'd never shown it to him in life and now she wished she'd had. There were many things she wished she'd said to her father.

When they rejoined Alex and Edmund, Pierre was with them.

"Etta," he said warmly, opening his arms. She hugged him as she never had before. Pierre and Maiya were all she had left of her father.

Alex had a grim look on his face as she approached. "My father was right," he said. "Magic is evil. I will do my best to crush it." He glanced around at the others in the room. "This I promise you."

Etta exchanged a look with Edmund, a silent conversation that needed no words.

Alex spun toward the door. "We should be out there fighting the bastards." Red crept up his neck as he tried to contain his anger.

Pierre shot Etta a pleading look.

"Your Majesty, there's nothing you can do."

A scream from the street pierced the air before it was abruptly cut off.

Alex glanced wildly between the door and Etta's calm face. He tore his eyes from her and made it to the door before they could stop him. "They're my people," he growled, yanking it open. "I will not hide while they are cut down."

"Shit." Edmund pulled his sword from its scabbard before looking to Etta. "I guess we're doing this." He rushed after Alex.

Etta took a step to follow them.

"They're your people, Persinette," Pierre said to her back. "Don't forget that as your sword cuts them down."

She didn't turn to look at him. "I don't have a choice. They may be my people, but I'm the cursed one. I fear my life will be spent fighting those I should be fighting for."

She ducked out the door and immediately found Edmund and Alex. They were locked in a battle with a man who was shooting sparks from his fingertips. They stood no chance. Etta ran around the side of the building, hidden from view, and called her magic forth. The stones beneath their feet began to shake and crack as they rose up. Alex stumbled back, his eyes wide. Edmund used the momentary break to push a burst of air at their attacker. He rose up slightly before slamming back against the face of the building.

Alex was too stunned to see Edmund's power. Etta ran forward as if she'd just arrived. Vérité joined her.

"We can't stay out here in the open," she said.

"You two need to get out of here." Edmund gestured to the horse.

"How?" Alex's eyes were still wild, but his breathing returned to normal. "They'll have blocked the road back to the palace."

"Go North."

"But that's ..."

"Through the Black Forest," Etta finished for him, shaking her head. She couldn't take the King of Gaule through the forest. For one, it wouldn't be safe. For him or the people that lived there. It was too close, too risky. Her secrets hung by a thread and Edmund was asking her to expose them even more.

"It's the only way." He glanced down the ally as footsteps reached their ears.

Etta shook herself. "What about you?"

"I'll be fine as long as the king is safe. You're his protector. So, protect."

They shared another one of their unspoken conversations, knowing they'd both risk it all to keep Alex safe. For him, it was love, loyalty. For her, it was the curse, but it was becoming so much more. After a lifetime preparing to hate him, she couldn't grasp the feelings swirling inside of her.

"Come on." She swung up into the saddle, motioning for the king to climb up behind her. He had no more objections. It was written in his eyes. He was no match for the magic these people held. He never would be.

As soon as he was up, Etta gathered the reins and Vérité took off without prompting. They cantered through the eerily empty and broken streets. The sounds of fighting from the market center died on the wind until all they heard was the steady drumming of the horse's hooves.

Neither of them spoke as they left the town behind them and rode on. The ride was long, and the forest stretched before them, shadowy and impenetrable. Only now, it was no longer protected. It was no longer held ghostly voices that echoed among the trees, or guarded the people hidden among the wards. Now they were visible. Their houses there for everyone to see.

Etta longed to go back to a simple time among the trees. Training with her father. Rides with Vérité. She could sense the horse's excitement as they neared.

Alex, on the other hand, tightened his grip on her. He'd been raised on stories from the forest. To him, it must have represented everything that was evil in Gaule.

He sucked in a breath loudly.

"You'll be okay," she said.

"I know that, but it doesn't make me any less desirous to be here. I should be heading back to the palace or fighting in the town."

"You'd never make it." She touched his hand gently. "You can't be a good king if you die before getting the chance to try."

His teeth ground together. "How long will we be in the woods?"

She thought for a moment, considering how far out of the way they'd have to go to avoid where she knew people lived. She wouldn't reveal them to the king for expediency's sake. "Maybe two days." Glancing at the waning sun behind her. "We entered at a far edge and will have to avoid all paths that lead into town or get any kind of traffic. It's around two days to the far side of the palace walls if we only take the safer paths."

"Safer paths?"

"Most of the stories about this place you've heard are ... untrue. But we still need to be cautious."

"How do you know so much about these woods?"

He was too close to the truth. Think. Think. She closed her eyes, thankful he couldn't see her face. "I used to hunt with my father here."

"You were brave."

She ignored that. If she were brave, she'd have ridden to Dracon to confront La Dame about breaking her curse instead of bowing to it.

Etta looked over her shoulder, considering if it was safe enough to stop. "Vérité needs a break." They were as safe as they could be after an attack in the village. She sighed and slid down. Alex followed her.

"I think we should travel without stopping," Alex said. "I need to get back to the palace as soon as possible to deal with the attackers and lend support to the village." He spoke rapidly. "Where did they come from? Are they working for La Dame? How many did they kill? Did they take hostages?"

"Slow down, your Majesty." She scanned the surrounding forest. "I know you've been relatively sheltered most of your life, but we can't be stupid. If we travel straight through, we'll be no use to anyone when we show up. We should find a place to set up camp soon. We'll need something to eat as well."

He considered her for a long moment, the side of his mouth quirking up. "Are you giving me—the king—orders?"

"Out here, there is no king, only the ones who survive and the ones who don't."

"I didn't know you had a bossy side. I've seen angry. Quiet. Unsure. Even kind. Never bossy."

She pushed by him, bumping his shoulder as she hid her smile from him.

"I like bossy."

They avoided any houses they passed, keeping to the paths Etta knew only too well. When she'd lived there, she'd avoided any contact with the others residing among the trees. Or maybe they'd avoided her. Whichever it was, she'd spent most of her time alone. Her father was always off, secretly watching the king from afar. The king he hated with everything he was. The king he'd never truly stopped serving.

The image of her father as his back hit the dirt played through her mind. She wiped away an angry tear before Alex could see how this place affected her. Her magic buzzed in a way it never did inside the castle walls, surrounded by her concrete prison. Out here, she knew every leaf, every flower that struggled to bloom. They called to her.

As the light faded, the trees became shadows, wrapping the travelers in a cloak of darkness. A warm night breeze lifted the hair off her neck and she turned, half expecting to see Edmund there, running to catch up. There was no one but Etta and the king, something she was acutely aware of.

"Etta." Alex's soft voice echoed through the space. "If you insist on us resting, we should find a place before we lose anymore light."

"Not yet." It was a dangerous thing to countermand a king, yet she continued to walk, pulling Vérité along behind her. They were close, she could feel it.

Her eyes lifted as they crested a hill, her glen laid out before them. A sigh hissed from her lips as relief flooded through her. She was home.

Her old shack was nowhere near, but this place meant more to her than her home ever had. The ground was soft under her feet and her eyes only caught the outlines of flowers stretching into the distance. But she didn't need to see them. She felt them.

"We're staying here for the night." She removed her scabbard and mail shirt. Her shoulders flexed as they enjoyed their freedom.

A drop of water hit her face, and she tilted it up to watch more break through the tree cover. She smiled despite herself.

Alex stopped beside her, droplets landing in his hair. "Just our luck."

She turned to face him.

He sucked in a breath. "I don't think I've ever seen you smile like that."

"You haven't known me long, your Majesty." She slipped into formality to put some distance between them. "Our time together has been fraught with turmoil. Even now. I shouldn't smile under these circumstances. I apologize." She dropped her gaze.

"No." He lifted his hand to trace the outline of the frown she now wore. "Please. When you smile, I feel like my entire world isn't crumbling down. Just for one moment." He snatched his hand back. "I just ..."

She looked to him, still torn between wanting to be rid of him forever and wanting something ... different. Maybe the key to the curse was not giving in to its demands, but in realizing she could make demands of it. She couldn't ignore it any longer. Whether it was the curse, that damn kiss, or something much, much more. She was drawn to this enemy of hers and she was tired of fighting it.

They both acted in the same moment. She gripped his shoulders as he slammed his mouth against hers. Desperation tugged at her. The rain began to come faster as her lips parted and his tongue met hers in a wave of ecstasy, a wave of fantasy. Because that's all it could ever be. Away from the castle, in the depths of her forest, a fantasy was born. They weren't ancient enemies. He knew her full name and everything she could do. And he was still there, kissing her as if none of it mattered.

A sob threatened to break their kiss because it did matter. If he knew, he'd have her hauled away.

He moaned into her mouth, pressing closer, and she pushed down her wretched despair. Gripping the edge of his shirt, she bunched it in her hands and skimmed the skin just beneath. He broke away from her long enough to tug it over his head.

His chest was slick with rain as she traced his muscles, warm under her hands.

"Etta," he growled.

It was pointless to try to stop as his mouth claimed hers once again.

"I've wanted you since the very first time I saw you at that tournament." His words vibrated against her lips.

She didn't tell him of the naive girl who'd, once upon a time, had a crush on a prince who was so very kind to her. She hadn't yet known how his fate would be tied to hers.

So, she tied it further.

It didn't matter that none of it was real—what he was feeling. It only mattered that for the first time since the tournament, she felt something other than the hole where her soul should be.

He captured her lips again as he pulled her down to the soft earth, pinning her beneath him. A puddle formed around them, but neither noticed as a stillness entered their hearts. Joined as one, the curse's constant pull fell silent.

None of it could last though and she'd never been more thankful for the darkness that hid her tears.

CHAPTER 16

A shiver ran the length of Alex's body as a groan from his empty stomach woke him. The sun was beginning to rise, obscured by the trees overhead. It took him a while to get his bearings, and then it all came flooding back to him. He sat up with a start. They'd been attacked the day before. He'd been forced to flee like a coward. Being king held no power when faced with magic.

He scrubbed a hand across his face and opened his eyes as two new realizations hit him. He was naked. And he was alone. They'd been soaking wet by the time they took cover from the rain in a dense patch of trees. All through the night, water dripped down onto them, but they'd used each other to stay warm.

Etta.

Where was she? His eyes scanned his surroundings. In the light, he could see for the first time where she'd brought him. Wild flowers of varying colors stretched in every direction. He climbed to his feet to get a better look and sucked in a breath at the beauty before him.

Nothing like this was supposed to exist in the Black Forest. It was supposed to be haunted, dangerous. But nothing was as it was supposed to be anymore.

Etta was no longer only his protector. There'd been a moment the night before when he felt her cede complete control, complete trust, and he'd done the same. There was no doubt in his mind that he loved her. He had since the very first time his eyes met her fierce ones.

But he was king.

He shook his head to clear the fog he felt creeping in and searched the ground for his discarded clothing. His pants were still sopping wet and now covered in dirt. He had no choice but to put them on. His shirt was a different matter. It lay on the ground, not two feet from where Vérité was tied.

Holding out a hand in front of him as a sign of friendship, he edged closer. The horse threw his head back, his mane catching in the breeze. He snorted and stamped his feet.

"Come on, Vérité," Alex said cautiously. "I thought we made progress yesterday when you saved my life." He bent to retrieve the shirt, but before his fingers could latch on to the fabric, Vérité snapped his teeth and the king jumped back in surprise.

"Vérité," he snapped. "I am your king. You will do as I say. Let me have my shirt."

The horse's nose flared, and he lurched forward with another snap of his teeth, almost nipping his king's arm.

"Treasonous bastard." Giving up on his shirt, Alex turned to go find Etta.

She was kneeling among a patch of bright yellow flowers with her head bent. Her words carried toward him.

"Father," she said. "This is so much harder than I thought it'd be. Things are falling apart."

Alex edged closer. Getting a glimpse into the real Etta was a rarity he couldn't pass up.

"I'm so lost. I don't know how to tell the difference between what I feel and what is being forced upon me."

Forced upon her? He thought about last night. Did she think she couldn't refuse him because he was king?

"I wish you were here to guide me." She got to her feet revealing a pile of stones that marked a gravesite.

She turned and her eyes widened upon seeing him. He suddenly felt like he'd intruded on an intensely private moment.

Etta wanted people to see her as a warrior. Someone without emotion. Without regret. She kept her past hidden.

But in that place, in that moment, her eyes held a vulnerability that nearly broke him. He closed the distance between them and pulled her against his chest, his arms wrapping around her back to keep her there. For once, she didn't resist the tie between them. Instead, she sank into it, pressing her face to his bare shoulder and breathing in deeply.

Their touch felt more intimate than what they'd done the night before. Their breath lined up, perfectly in sync, as they took comfort in one another.

"Are you okay?" Alex asked softly.

"No," she replied.

"Did you know them?" He gestured to the grave. He already knew the answer, but he wanted her to confide in him.

She pulled back to look at him.

He brushed the blond hair from her face as she hesitated.

Finally, she nodded. "My father."

"I have so many questions about you, Etta."

"Please." She pressed her cheek back to his chest. "Don't ask them. I don't want to lie to you."

He shook his head. "I'm the King of Gaule and I can't even get my protector to share her family name. Her father is mysteriously buried in the Black Forest. I don't know how she learned to fight or why. All I know is that I feel drawn to her, like kissing her gives me life."

"Is that enough?" The question was no more than a whisper.

He kissed the top of her head and spoke into her hair. "For now, but not forever."

She broke away from him. "We should get going. You are needed at the palace." She stopped walking when she reached Vérité and her fingers worked to untie him.

She bent down to retrieve Alex's shirt. "Missing something?"

"Damn horse wouldn't let me near it."

Etta shook her head, the hint of a smile appearing on her lips. "Will you two ever stop fighting?"

"It's his fault."

"Sure, your Majesty." She lifted the saddle and slid it into place before he could help her. As she reached below to buckle it, she glanced back at him. "I'd put that shirt on if I were you. We can't have the king showing up at the palace half-naked."

He laughed and pulled it on over his head, hoping it would dry quickly.

Etta climbed up and Vérité stomped his foot as Alex tried to do the same.

"Stop that." Etta smacked the horse's neck, and he stopped long enough for the king to pull himself up.

Then he took off. As Alex looked back, part of him didn't want to leave that place behind. A tranquil peace existed among the trees that would be gone as soon as they were far away. Because he knew. When he made it home, he'd be returning to a country at war.

Urgency made the trip long. Vérite could only canter for so long before slowing.

The air surrounding them was fresh and clean from the night's rain. It was full of life, but Alex could only focus on the woman in front of him. Her warmth was nestled between his thighs, and his arm rose and fell against her stomach with each breath she took. She shook her head and her golden braid fell over one shoulder. He pushed the remaining hairs aside and pressed his lips to the back of her neck. She leaned into him.

"Alex," she breathed. "Last night was…"

"Perfect?"

She shook her head and when he ran his hands down the lengths of her arms, she shivered.

"Stop smiling," she said.

His laugh rumbled against her back. "How do you know I'm smiling?"

She twisted in the saddle to look back at him and touched the dimples in his cheeks. His smile widened. "I know you, Alex."

She dropped her hand and turned back around as if she'd said something she shouldn't and Alex didn't stop her. She was holding back from him and soon they'd return to the palace where he'd have to be king and she'd be his protector. There was a storm awaiting them. Flashes of the battle the day before played in his mind as he closed his eyes.

Edmund would be okay. They'd left him in the middle of the fight, but he could protect himself. They'd walked through the gates and he'd be waiting with a grin on his face, a misplaced grin after an attack, but it would suit him.

What of the people in the village? The healer and his daughter who'd helped them? The people in the market square who'd come out just to get a glimpse of their king?

"The attack is only the beginning, isn't it?"

He didn't realize he'd spoken aloud until Etta responded. "I didn't always think the wards were a just means of defense." She paused. "I don't know how freely I can speak to the king."

He spread his fingers across the flat plains of her stomach. "Say what you wish."

She was quiet for a long moment. "Your father wasn't a good king."

"You didn't know him."

She hesitated. "No, but I know this country a little better than you."

He took his hands from her. "I am the king," he growled.

Verite snorted and he would have sworn the horse didn't appreciate his tone.

"You said I could say anything," she said boldly. "I will not indulge you in useless flattery."

He breathed deeply to calm the defensive words on his tongue. "Go on."

"Your father was a tyrant who hunted his own people. The wards allowed him to do that without any avenue for them to escape. Any with magic in their blood could not cross the border. It kept Gaule safe, but it also cut the country off from the outside world. Those without magic didn't cross for fear of capture."

"A very real threat."

She nodded. "I know and that is why my heart is torn. The wards imprisoned magic folk, but kept everyone else safe. La Dame is out there."

"I saw her once," he said.

Etta went still. "How?"

"It was before the wards were put up. I was only a boy and my father took me to the border. She was our ally."

"Why would she ally with Gaule?"

Alex shrugged. "I've been wondering that myself. She's ancient and power emanates from her every pore."

"What was she like?" Etta's voice held a hint of fear, the first fear Alex had seen from her.

"Wonderful."

Etta shifted. "Wonderful?"

"And terrifying. She didn't look much older than I am now, but what I remember most were her eyes. When I looked into them, all that I was, all that I'd ever be was rendered unimportant. There was only her. I lost any sense of myself. All I wanted was to please her." He leaned his chin on Etta's shoulder. "It was both the best and worst day of my life."

Etta laced her fingers with his where they rested against her stomach and snapped the reigns with her other hand.

"It's okay," she whispered. "You were just a child."

"I shouldn't have been so enchanted. She did the same thing to my father. I heard the guards talking the next morning about how my father had been found in her bed. He had many mistresses, but that night changed him. It struck a fear in him. As we were leaving, a voice sounded in my mind."

"What did it say?"

He squeezed her tighter against him, needed her warmth to push away the numbness brought on by the memories. "She told me I'd come back to her one day. It didn't matter. The next day, my father had Viktor construct the wards."

Etta gasped as the realization came to her. "The wards were the ultimate betrayal."

"Yes, Etta, when you said my father was a horrible king, you didn't know how right you were. He betrayed the most powerful woman in the world. A woman who has destroyed greater men and brought entire kingdoms to their knees. And he had Viktor use his magic to prevent her from setting foot in this kingdom again."

"And Viktor helped him," Etta whispered. "They left us with this."

"She's going to come for us," he said. "The question is when. I think we still have time to prepare. When she makes a move, it will be calculated, planned. Look at the legends of Bela. If those are to be believed, her plan took generations to complete."

"The difference," Etta began. "Is that Bela had its own source of power. The people had magic, just like La Dame's people in Dracon. Gaule doesn't stand a chance."

"While I am king, it will always have a chance."

They left the woods at the edge of the Black Forest, nearest the far side of the castle walls in the late afternoon. Neither of them knew the state of the little town behind those walls. It wasn't safe for the king to show up at the front gate.

"We have to separate," Etta said as they neared the walls.

Alex led them to a hidden door that went mostly unused. There was no need for secrecy in times of peace.

"Not a chance."

"Vérité can't enter that way and I'm not leaving him. As soon as you're inside the inner palace, you'll be safe."

"What about you?"

"We don't know the outer palace has been compromised." Her eyes roamed the length of the walls.

"We don't know it hasn't."

"This is non-negotiable, your Highness."

"You don't give me orders," he growled in irritation.

"I do when it comes to your safety. My job is to protect you and that means getting you somewhere safe, regardless of my own safety."

He started to argue, but she reached down to grip the hand he had on her stomach as they rode up the grassy hill. Her fingers threaded between his and he squeezed.

It still wasn't real to her—everything she was feeling. It was a part of the curse. But she no longer cared. For the first time since her father died, she didn't feel completely and utterly alone. She wanted the feeling to last until the time came for her to break the curse. That was still the mission, even if it took her entire life to do it.

And when it was gone, the King of Gaule would marry his betrothed, the decorative, highborn Amalie. If they all survived that long.

They dismounted as they came up alongside the tall, outer wall of the castle. Etta glanced up. "Once inside that door, there's a secret passage that'll take you past the inner wall."

"How do you know that?"

"Your brother told me all about his tunnels and passages."

That made him smile.

She walked him toward the door, her eyes scanning for trouble, hand on the hilt of her sword.

Alex brought their joined hands to his lips and kissed them before looking down at her. "Promise me that inside those walls, nothing will change."

She removed her hand. "You are the king."

"Nice of you to notice."

She bit her lower lip. "It's the palace. Inside those walls, everything changes."

His shoulders sagged in resignation as he put a hand to the door to push it open. "I need you safe. If anything happens to you, it'll kill me."

Literally, she thought.

But he didn't know that. So, she hardened her eyes and pressed her lips together. "I am your protector, your Majesty, not the other way around."

Hurt flashed in his eyes and then he was gone, leaving Etta on that grassy hill outside the walls with only her temperamental horse for company.

"Come on, boy." She hooked her foot into a stirrup and pulled herself up before swinging her leg over his back. "Let's see what kind of mess we're walking into."

Vérité jerked his head to the side as Etta slid her sword free. He wasn't used to weapons yet. They cantered the length of the wall, turning toward the massive steel gates that stood as a barrier to those wanting to break through.

Closed? They never closed the outer gates.

Hoping it meant they hadn't been attacked, she nudged Vérité forward. As she neared, a line of soldiers appeared atop the wall, bows in hands. The tips of their arrows were aimed directly at her.

There was no doubt in her mind, they could take her down in one shot. Gaule's archers shot true.

She infused steel into her voice as she raised her gaze. "Open the gates."

A man pushed through the line of archers to look down at her. She recognized him immediately. Anders. Could he recognize her from afar?

"Who demands entry?"

Well, that answered that question.

She drew herself up, sitting as straight as she could. "I am Etta, Protector of King Alexandre."

A beat of silence passed. Then another.

"Put away your sword," Anders demanded.

She did as she was bid, and watched the heavy gates open slowly.

Anders rushed down the steps to meet her. She slid from Vérité's back as the gates closed behind them.

"Where is the king?" Anders demanded, his harsh eyes boring into hers.

"Safe," she responded. "He should be in the inner palace by now."

"You shouldn't have separated him from his guards during the attack."

"I didn't separate him. The men and women attacking us did."

"He's been presumed dead. You both have."

She studied him, unable to tell if Anders was satisfied they were alive or not. "Your son could have told you we escaped."

He scowled and a flash of pain crossed his face. "Edmund is no son of mine." With that, he turned and stomped off, his steel-toed boots slamming against the stone road.

What is going on?

Etta gripped Vérité's reins tightly in her fist and tugged him along behind her. The soldiers at the gate returned to their watch, not looking at her as she went by. The streets were deserted, an uncommon sight while the sun still hung in the sky.

Occasionally, a head would poke out of a house or a shop she passed, but they always ducked away in fear. Who were they afraid of behind these walls?

In the silence, the sound of someone running toward her was deafening. The armor-clad soldier stopped when she reached Etta.

"Protector," she said, inclining her head. "The king sent me to fetch the horse so you could go straight to the palace."

Etta nodded, ceding the reins gratefully. "Fill me in on the way."

The girl didn't need further explanation. "The village is all but destroyed. Many lost their lives. The others seek refuge behind our walls."

"How did the palace fare?"

"We were not attacked. By the time the royal guard was ready to move toward the village, the magic wielders were already gone. We lined the walls in wait, but nothing ever came."

"Who were the attackers working for?"

"As far as we can tell, themselves. There seems to be no outside force involved."

It was La Dame. It had to be. She refused to believe the magic community in Gaule would sanction such bloodshed.

They reached the stables and Etta nodded a goodbye to her before quickening her steps. She breathed more easily once she was past the inner gates and into the training yard.

Tyson was sitting in the courtyard on the steps leading to the large doors with his head in his hands. He started as Etta neared and jumped to his feet.

He ran forward and threw his arms around her. "Thank you for keeping him safe."

"I'll always protect him." She let him hug her for a moment longer before pulling back.

"I know you will." He wiped at his face to try to hide his tears. There was an innocence to Tyson that she feared would soon be broken. Just as Alex's was all those years ago.

He stepped back, suddenly self-conscious. "Mother told me to wait for you out here. Alex is in there throwing things."

"Why would he do that?"

His eyes dropped, and he sank back down on the steps. The next three words out of his mouth sliced through her like the sharp edge of a knife.

"Edmund's been arrested."

CHAPTER 17

Etta's feet carried her through the empty palace halls. The servants hid in alcoves near the kitchen and she knew why. The king's screams permeated the walls.

She followed the sounds to the throne room where two guards waited outside a closed door.

"Open it," she demanded. "Now."

They didn't hesitate in letting her through before closing it behind her.

Alex stood against the wall, near a table laden with food and drink for those in attendance. His mother stood a fair distance away, as did Princess Camille. Various lords and ladies watched him warily.

He had yet to bathe or change, his clothing still crusty with the same dirt that streaked through his hair. He did not look like a king.

A roar ripped through the room as Alex threw a goblet against the wall. It shattered and burgundy wine ran down the stone.

No one made a move to clean it up. Etta's eyes took in the room, noting that it wasn't the first thing he'd thrown.

His face reddened as he took two heavy steps toward a guard who was cowering near him. "Lies," he spat. "You speak lies."

He shook as he averted his eyes from the irate king. "Sire. We have many accounts."

Alex growled. "Get out of my sight."

The guard ran from the room as if chased.

Etta stepped up next to Queen Catrine. The queen's face relaxed in relief. "You're here."

Etta nodded.

"Thank you for bringing him back."

Etta watched Alex pace the room as she spoke to his mother. "What has Edmund done?"

"Eyewitnesses say he was using magic during the attack."

She bit down on her lip as all the possibilities raced through her mind. God, Edmund. Did they know about her? What would they do to him? A lot of that would depend on the king who was currently growling at anyone who looked his way.

She leaned closer to the queen. "But he only used it to save the king."

If Catrine was surprised Etta knew about Edmund's magic, she didn't show it. "That doesn't matter in Gaule. Just possessing the magic is a crime punishable by death."

"Alex wouldn't ..."

"Alexandre was raised by a man who had his own protector hunted." She looked toward her son. "I honestly don't know what he'll do. He must keep his nobles content."

Before Etta could respond, Camille stepped forward, her words to her brother ringing throughout the room. "Brother, you know the punishment for magic."

Etta couldn't stay quiet any longer. "Alex, it's Edmund."

"Your Majesty," Camille snapped.

"What?"

"You will address the king as 'your Majesty' as befits your position, Protector."

Etta narrowed her eyes. "Your Majesty, Edmund saved your life in the attack."

"How do we know he wasn't a part of it?" Camille asked. "Wasn't it Edmund who pushed to go into town?"

"Attack or not, going to the people was the right thing to do. A king cannot rule if he does not know them." Etta pinned the princess with a stare.

Camille marched toward Etta and glared into her eyes. Etta wanted to push her away, but to lay hands on the princess was a crime.

"You're just a protector. Your knowledge goes no further than the tip of your sword. Don't pretend it does."

"And your knowledge, Princess, ends at pretty dresses."

Etta's cheek stung before she even saw the princess draw her hand back in preparation for the slap. The sound of their flesh meeting clapped through the space.

Jaws hung open around the room, but Etta remained still. She couldn't react. That was what Camille wanted.

She stared into the girl's cruel eyes as all air left the room.

Then Camille disappeared. Alex stood behind her, several feet away, gripping her shoulders. He shoved her, and she stumbled before righting herself.

Etta lifted her eyes to the king, but he didn't meet them. Instead, he walked by her, slamming the door open and leaving them all in shock.

"Etta, dear," the queen said. "Go."

She was right. Her job was to be at his side whether he wanted anyone there or not. Now was not the time for him to be wandering the palace alone.

She followed him, not sparing one more thought for the people she left behind.

Alex tore through his room, rage rising up from the pit of his stomach. How had he missed it? His entire life, Edmund had been there. When magic was purged from the realm, he'd stayed. He was the captain of the guard's son. If magic passed down through blood, how did it get into his?

It must have been his mysterious mother.

The bookshelf by the door shook as he slammed his foot into it, scattering books across the floor. He needed something to hit, someone to take the blame.

This could not be happening.

He flipped open his sketchpad, the first page showing Edmund sitting proudly atop a horse in full armor. He'd been sixteen at the time and allowed Alex to use him for drawing practice—back when Alex was under the delusion that it was okay for a future king to skip his training to hide away with his sketchpad.

A smile stretched Edmund's face. It wasn't the best drawing, but the joy was there. He was his best friend, his brother.

And he'd lied to him their whole lives.

He was tainted. Evil.

Nothing about magic could be good. Not when they attacked his villages.

His best friend was nothing more than an enemy in disguise.

A cry lodged in his throat as he tore the page to shreds and threw the book across the room as hard as he could. It landed with a thud right in front of two worn boots. His eyes traveled up to find Etta watching him. She cocked her head, her eyes showing the only sign of weariness from their journey.

They had no time for weariness.

She bent to pick up the sketchbook before walking forward to set it on the table beside him.

"You should go." It came out more as a sigh than the growl he'd intended.

"I am your protector."

"There's nothing to protect me from in here."

"There's plenty."

Alex walked across the room and sank onto the edge of the bed, leaning forward with his elbows on his knees. His dark hair spilled forward, covering the torture in his eyes.

"My best friend is sitting in my dungeon." The words released from him in one long stream as if an admittance of guilt.

What was he guilty of?

Not hating the man who'd been like a brother to him? Failing to act swiftly to rid Gaule of his magic?

"He's not the man I thought he was."

Etta dropped to her knees in front of him. "Of course he is. He's the same man who risked his life entering the tournament, just for a chance to be at your side."

He tore his gaze from hers and stood abruptly, the anger from before returning.

"How could you say those words to me? Edmund is no better than the people who attacked us in the village, no better than the man who killed my father."

Etta rocked back to sit on her heels, not rising to face him.

Why wasn't she agreeing with him? The opinionated Etta was quiet, avoiding his eyes. When he was a lad, and his playmate possessed the magic, he'd sometimes envied her. He wanted to feel that power. But that was before. Before they flocked to La Dame's forces and tried to ruin Gaule. Before they were hunted down by his father.

He'd ridden out toward the end of the purge when there were few prisoners left to take. His father had forced him. Edmund hadn't been there. Why hadn't he found that strange?

How hadn't he known?

"I need to see him," Alex said, moving toward the door.

"Now?" Etta hurried after him. "You aren't in the right mind for this." She moved to block him. "Maybe you need a bath, dinner, and some sleep. He'll still be there in the morning."

"Move, Etta, before I make you."

She took in the stubbornness on his face and stepped aside. It was as if the night before was a distant memory. An icy chill returned between them as they walked through the palace, the king and his protector. Servants bowed and scurried out of the way to avoid the fierceness of his gaze.

The dungeons were across the palace. They descended the sharp, narrow staircase as the air grew cooler, and moisture stuck to their skin. Lanterns hung along the walls, casting a dim, yellow light across the darkness. Two guards sat at the bottom of the stairs with a table between them.

One cheered as a pair of dice clacked together, but the other spotted the king and stood immediately.

"Sire." He said as the other guard finally noticed them and jumped to his feet.

"Take me to the magic man."

They turned and led Etta and Alex down a long hall. Cells lined each wall, most of them full of poor, wretched people. Alex couldn't look as their moans and pleas reached his ears.

Most of these people had been arrested by his father, their crimes unknown to Alex. But he only had his sights on one criminal.

They turned the corner into another room in the labyrinth beneath the palace. Only one cell there was occupied.

Edmund sat against the wall, chains keeping him in place. His legs were spread wide in front of him and bent at the knee. He rested his arms on his knees and hung his head.

Without lifting his eyes, he spoke.

"Come to tell me my fate, your Majesty?"

Edmund's fair blond hair was matted with blood that streaked down the side of his face, drying in clumps. A purple bruise stretched across his jaw.

He finally raised his eyes, still not acknowledging Alex. Instead, he looked to Etta, and the chains rattled as he lifted a hand to touch his jaw gently. "It's okay, Etta. I deserved it."

Etta shook her head. He didn't deserve any of it.

As if reading her thoughts, he smiled slightly. "I may have resisted arrest a little."

Alex stepped forward to grip the bars of his friend's prison. "How could you?"

"How could I what?" He finally snapped his eyes to his king's. "Be what I was born? Keep it a secret when I spent all my teenage years listening to how much you and your father hated my people?" Fire burned in his eyes, but also something else. Betrayal?

Alex would be too blind to see it, but Etta recognized the source of Edmund's anger. Love. Alex meant everything to him and now they stood on opposite sides of prison bars.

"Edmund," Etta said softly. "Why don't you show him what you can do. Show him that it isn't something evil."

When she tried to put a hand on Alex's arm, he jerked away from her and turned his accusing stare on her, realizing for the first time that she knew.

"You," he said.

"I didn't want this to happen to him." Panic clawed at her throat. How much more was she going to accidentally reveal? It could have just as easily been her in the dungeons. Edmund shot her a warning glance. She reached for Alex's hand and this time he let her take it. "I couldn't put that on you." She nodded to Edmund. "Do it."

The world around them quieted in an instant. The moans from the other prisoners faded away and it was just the three of them. A small wind blew through the enclosed room and Alex jumped, his eyes rounding. His mouth moved as if trying to speak, but words failed him.

Etta squeezed his hand as Edmund pulled his magic back. The wind stopped abruptly.

Alex shook his head, incredulous as he stared at Edmund, a new distrust in his eyes. Before, he'd only heard about it. Now, he'd seen his friend's power for himself.

"I've felt that before," the king admitted. "Many times." His eyes zeroed in on Edmund. "You've used your magic on me."

"It wasn't like that." Edmund scrambled to his knees and moved closer until his chains tugged him back. His anger was gone, replaced with desperation.

He needed his friend to understand, but Etta knew better. A Durand would never understand. She released Alex's hand. That was why they were enemies of the Basiles. The fantasy of the last day shattered around her as she saw what could never be.

"Alex," Edmund pleaded. "You're the only thing in my life I care about. You have enemies, but I am not one of them. I want to help keep you safe."

"You are wrong, Edmund." Alex turned away. "You became my enemy the day you were born."

A sob tore from Edmund's chest as Alex walked away from him without a single glance back. Etta stayed rooted to the spot, her eyes never leaving the broken man in front of her.

"How are we supposed to keep him safe if he won't let us?" she asked.

"Stay hidden, Etta. He needs you."

"He needs both of us." She watched him for a moment longer. "I love him too, you know."

He burned his eyes into her. "Then we're both screwed."

CHAPTER 18

I love him too, you know.

They'd been her words, coming unbidden and unwelcome. Etta tried to tell herself they were to comfort Edmund. That they hid some deeper meaning about protecting the king.

She couldn't love a Durand. She couldn't even be friends with one.

Her footsteps followed closely behind Alex as he made his way to his room, his head ducked to avoid looking at anyone they passed. She felt for the comfort of her sword at her side, brushing the back of her hand across the hilt.

Alex's guards opened the double doors to his rooms, and he walked through before turning back to her. Gone was the anger of only moments before. His tired eyes held hers for just a moment before he sighed.

"Goodnight, Protector."

His formality struck a pain in her chest, but she managed a short bow. "Your Majesty."

The door slammed shut, leaving her staring at the solid wood in front of her face.

That was how it should've been. The king and his protector. Formality kept a distance between them, a distance they'd breached when everything in her said it was a bad idea.

Squaring her shoulders, she turned, ignoring the curious looks from the guards at the king's door. Her feet took her down the hall to the room she'd been granted, near the king. Never far.

In case someone needed to fight for him.

Not for her to feel his body against hers.

She shut the door behind her and leaned her back up against it, closing her eyes as a long breath forced past her teeth.

She opened them and pushed away from the door to look around her room. The maids had been there in her absence. Her bed was made. The room was spotless. As she walked forward, she scanned the tray they'd left for her. Hunks of bread and cheese with thin slices of meat sat beside a pitcher and two cups. She grabbed a piece of bread and sank teeth into it, her stomach rumbling in anticipation. She hadn't eaten since the day before.

The trip through the Black Forrest seemed like a lifetime ago. So much had happened since then, so much had changed.

Her fingers closed around the cool handle of the copper pitcher as she lifted it to pour a cup of water. The water soothed her aching throat.

Water trickled down her chin as she gulped it before setting the empty cup down, too tired to eat more. She wiped her mouth with the back of her hand and made her way to the bathing area where a bath had been drawn. Sticking one finger into the full tub, a smile curved her lips at finding it still warm.

Etta's sheathed sword clunked when she unbuckled it and let it fall to the ground.

She bent at the waist and pulled her mail shirt over her head, feeling lighter for it. The rest of her clothes followed to the pile on the ground before she stepped into the tub and sank down with a sigh. The water enveloped her, soothing every ache except the one in her heart.

Did she deserve to enjoy this while Edmund was in the dungeon? It could just as well be her.

The answer never came, but she was too tired to care.

Sliding lower, she dipped below the water, letting the rest of the world fade away. When she finally broke the surface again, she gasped for air.

Holding her hands in front of her face, she examined them. Each line. Each digit. They held so much power. Power that could destroy her.

If this day had taught her anything, it was that she couldn't stay in Gaule. It was time to search for something that could break the curse.

A scar ran up the side of Etta's right arm, her sword arm. She fingered it, knowing it was not unlike the scars on her back. Had Alex seen them? One could not become a master with the sword without suffering for it. Her father taught her that. He hadn't held back, and neither had she.

But the deepest scar had nothing to do with a sword at all. It was on the back of her leg. When she was a child, young Prince Alexandre dared her to climb the outside of the north tower. Infatuated with him as she was, she agreed. She could climb anything. But she'd been caught and in an attempt to get away, she'd fallen, landing on one of the blacksmith's tools.

Her fingers traced the edge of the scar as memories overcame her. She closed her eyes to will them away.

Alex wasn't so lucky. Every time he closed his eyes, he was transported into the past. A past he now knew to be filled with lies.

"I'm Edmund." The gangly teen flipped his too-long blond hair out of his face and held out his hand to the prince, either forgetting or not knowing proper formalities.

Alex didn't mind. He hated all the titles and pretensions.

He took Edmund's hand and squeezed, their eyes meeting. Edmund grinned. It wouldn't be long before Alex learned that smiling was just his natural expression.

They released each other as Alex looked to his father who was speaking to the new captain of the guard, Edmund's father. They'd moved into the palace after Anders spent the past few years on assignment at the border.

The forces at the border had been reduced to almost nothing now that the wards were in place.

The wards. Viktor.

Persinette.

They'd been gone a week, and each day they weren't dragged back in chains lightened Alex's heart a bit. He missed his friend.

Guilt was a powerful emotion.

Even if Persinette wasn't found, plenty of other magic folk had been captured. Some imprisoned. Others executed.

Edmund seemed to sense a cloud hanging over Alex so he nudged his shoulder. "Think we can sneak out of this dreadfully boring meeting?"

Alex smiled and nodded slowly. No one noticed as the boys crept from the throne room and went running toward the inner gate of the castle.

"Where do you want to go?" Edmund asked.

Alex began leading them to the one place he wanted to be without even thinking about it. The North tower was unmanned, allowing them to approach. It was surrounded by the blacksmith's shop on one side and a grassy hill on the other.

Alex tilted his head back to peer up. "A friend of mine tried to climb the outside one time."

Edmund laughed. "That's like suicide."

"I may have dared her."

"A girl?"

His incredulous stare made Alex laugh. "She had no fear."

"I think I'd like to meet this girl, then."

Alex's eyes shuttered, all humor leaving as if it never existed at all. "She's gone."

Edmund thought for a moment. "I like you—even though you are a prince."

"I'm glad you can overlook my faults," Alex answered dryly.

"I think this is the point where I pledge myself to you or something? Isn't that what people do? I'm only fifteen, but already better than most with a sword." He puffed out his chest. "I don't want to serve your father like my dad. I'm hilarious. The girls can't resist my easy charm—but you're a prince, so they probably flock to you anyway."

As he listed his best qualities, Alex held in a laugh.

When he finally let it out, he shook his head. "Why don't you just be my friend?"

"Oh, that I can definitely do. I'm a very good friend."

Alex rolled over, a blinding headache jolting him from sleep.

When Edmund was selling himself, he'd failed to mention he represented everything the Durands were against.

He'd felt it. Edmund's magic. There was no denying it now.

He covered his head with his pillow and begged for unconsciousness to take him once more.

CHAPTER 19

Three heavy knocks jerked Etta awake. She'd fallen asleep in the tub and the water had long gone cold.

The persistent knocking grew louder.

It couldn't possibly be morning.

She stood, letting the water run from her body and stepped from the tub. A puddle formed at her feet. "One moment," she grumbled, lunging for a robe that hung on the end of her bed. She glanced out the window on her way by, noting the darkened sky and full moon still shining brightly.

Her footsteps quickened as she realized something urgent must have happened for someone to wake her at this hour. When she pulled open the door, her mouth fell open at the sight of Queen Catrine and Prince Tyson before her.

"Please," the dowager queen began. "Let us in before Alexandre's guards see us."

Still in shock, Etta stepped back. "Is everything okay? Has something happened?"

"Hold on." The queen scanned the hall once before stepping in and shutting the door. "We can't have anyone knowing we were here."

"I'm sorry, I don't understand."

"You will." She breezed through the room. "Do you have anything to eat? Poor Tyson has been hiding in my rooms for the better part of the night and I couldn't have anyone know he was there." She spotted the mostly full tray of food and wine and went to it. "That's why I had this sent here."

"My queen—" Etta began.

"Dear." The queen pinned her with a look. "You may as well call me Catrine. Tonight I must spill all my secrets to you."

"Why me?"

"You'll understand in a moment." She handed Tyson a piece of bread she'd slathered with jam and he attacked it hungrily.

Tyson looked ... different. His eyes darted around nervously. His clothing was a rumpled mess. All mischief was gone from his expression. Etta had never seen him look so ... scared. What was he scared of?

The queen poured herself a goblet of wine and then offered one to Etta. "Trust me, you're going to need it."

Etta accepted the cup and sipped hesitantly, her eyes never leaving mother and son. "Do I need to fetch Alexandre for this?"

Tyson's head snapped up at the same time his mother issued an emphatic "No!"

Warning bells rang in Etta's mind. She set her wine down and crossed her arms. "I take it I'll need to sit for this."

"Please," Catrine said. "It's going to be a long conversation."

Etta walked around to the front of the sofa and sat, her posture rigid. The silence stretched before them as Tyson continued to eat and Catrine closed her eyes as if gathering her will.

She studied her son. "Ty, are you ready?"

His eyes widened, but he set his food down and nodded. He poured himself a cup of water and clutched it in his hands as he walked forward.

His voice shook as he began speaking. "There's a tunnel from the castle that ends at the sea. I told Alex about it once, but I think he's forgotten. That's where I first learned what I could do."

"What you can do?" Etta leaned forward.

He lowered himself so his knees hit the stone floor and bent forward. Etta almost reached out to stop him as he deliberately poured the water onto the ground. It puddled in front of him.

He set the cup aside and raised a hand above the puddle. The water began to expand and spread. He didn't move as it slinked between his knees and before long, he was encircled.

Etta sucked in a breath as her head shook of its own accord. Her eyes had to have been deceiving her. A prince of Gaule couldn't have magic. He just couldn't.

The water continued to move, hitting the edge of the carpet beneath her bed and pushing up over it, moving through the rich fibers. The carpet darkened as it became saturated.

"How?" Etta whispered, sure no one else heard her.

Catrine watched her face for any reaction. All she must have seen was complete shock.

When the water hit the wall, Tyson flicked his hand, and it began to retract. The carpet became bright as it dried instantly. The puddle shrank and contracted, the molecules moving as a single organism. Finally, when it was back to its original size,

Tyson pushed it over the rim of the cup and it was as if it had never left at all.

Etta's legs shook under her as she got to her feet. Silently, she walked toward the bed and bent to run her fingers across the carpet. Completely dry.

She turned to the queen and prince who had so many secrets and asked the one question that terrified her more than any other.

"Why did you come to me?"

The air hung heavy with impending confessions and Etta found it harder to breathe with each passing second. So, the prince had magic. It was hard to even begin to comprehend what that meant.

Etta focused on the Queen, her question forgotten for the moment as realization struck her. The magic must run in Tyson's blood. One of his parents must have been a descendant of Bela just as she was. Or worse, Dracon.

"You have many questions, Etta," Catrine said. "Let's start at the beginning. I have brought my son to you because I know who you are."

Etta's heart pounded like a battering ram trying to rip through her chest.

Sympathy flooded Catrine's gaze, and she moved closer to Etta, placing a calming hand on her arm. "It's okay, Persinette." She smiled. "I have been wanting to call you that since the day my husband told me your true identity."

That day flashed through her mind. If the king hadn't been killed, she'd have been arrested and probably executed. After she won, and no one came for her, she assumed he hadn't shared his suspicions with anyone. But, of course, the queen knew.

When Etta sat paralyzed, Catrine went on. "I warned your father."

An emotion flashed in her eyes and Etta couldn't make sense of it.

"My father," Etta whispered.

Tears glistened in Catrine's eyes but didn't fall. "Viktor did the only thing he could to keep you safe."

"I know."

Catrine scrutinized her son who was listening avidly. "I wish you could have known Viktor Basile, but you were only a child when he left."

"He didn't leave." Steel entered Etta's voice. "His wife was murdered, and he was forced to flee with his daughter. Then he was hunted for years by the very man he'd served loyally."

Catrine wiped a hand across her face and seemed to grow older with every word she spoke. Her mouth turned down, and she glanced away. "He didn't deserve any of that."

"Does Alex know who you are?" Tyson asked suddenly.

She jerked her head up. "No. And he can't. Not ever. Just like he can't know about you."

"He's my brother."

"He's also the man who at this very moment has his best friend in the dungeons." Etta sighed. "He isn't a bad man, not like," she looked to Catrine then back to Tyson, "your father. But he's conflicted, and he thinks magic is evil."

"Isn't it?" A boyish vulnerability entered his voice and Etta couldn't take it. She got to her feet and went to crouch in front of him, forcing him to look her in the eyes.

"You are not evil." She sat back on her heels. "People will say differently, but it isn't the magic that makes a person good or bad. It's how they use it. You have a choice. Use it for good and you will be good."

Tyson nodded wordlessly and when she returned to her seat, Catrine shot her a grateful, almost proud, smile. There'd been a time when she'd idolized the queen. Her mother would take her to tea and she'd sit there in awe. That was before she began wanting to watch the guards in the training yard instead.

"Persinette." The queen said her name as if it was the most natural thing in the world. As if it didn't tug on Etta's heart to have someone, anyone, know who she really was.

"We came to you tonight because we need your help, but first, before I put another son's life in your hands, I have so many questions."

Etta knew this day would come, the day she'd need to reveal herself. Unexpected relief flooded through her at the thought of unburdening herself.

"I'll tell you everything I can," she promised

Catrine leaned closer and Tyson got up from where he still sat on the floor to perch on her other side, both eager for the truth.

"First," the queen said. "Tell me why you want to protect Alexandre."

Etta breathed deeply and began the only way she knew how. "It started with a curse."

She had their rapt attention, so the story spilled out of her.

"Many generations ago, when Queen Aurora of Bela was dying, she was put into a deep sleep. King Phillip knew that the only way to wake her and save her was a magical plant called rampion – some called it Rapunzel- that grew beyond the walls of Dracon. He took his men to procure it, but they were captured by La Dame, the very same La Dame who poses a threat across the border now."

Catrine sucked in a breath.

"Thinking it was an invasion—Phillip had brought a sizable legion of his army—her only thought was to destroy the royal line of Bela in the most painful way possible."

"A curse?" Tyson asked.

Etta nodded. "Aurora and Phillip could have the rapunzel, but they must give up their first born, a son. This prince, upon his eighteenth birthday, would go to serve as a protector to their greatest enemies, the Durands of Gaule."

"What does this have to do with you?"

"Giving up their son was not the cruelest part of the curse. Every generation until the end of the line would repeat the same process, the first born of each generation would serve the Durands. La Dame connected us. We can feel when our charges are far away. When they're hurt, we hurt." She paused, meeting Catrine's eyes. "When they die, we die."

"Viktor." Catrine lifted her hand to cover her mouth before pinning Etta with her gaze. "You and Alexandre?"

Etta nodded slowly.

The queen leaned forward, breaking the perfect posture she'd always had. Placing her elbows on her lap, she covered her face as her back began to shake.

And that's when Etta knew. She was watching a queen break right before her eyes. The people you worship as children seem as something other than human. They're strong, impenetrable. They aren't supposed to shatter like a pane of glass, leaving shards to mirror the destruction.

Tyson stood and moved closer to his mother before sitting beside her and folding her into his youthful arms.

Etta drained her wine, needing the heady buzz to keep from breaking down herself.

When Catrine finally lifted her eyes once again, her face was streaked with tears. "How much you must hate us, child."

Etta bristled. There was truth to those words. She did hate the Durands. She hated everything they stood for, everything they'd done. But the woman sitting in front of her was not her husband. And everything inside of her begged not to hate Alex.

"The Basiles and Durands are the greatest of enemies," she said carefully. "Bela may be no more, but its royal line lives on in me." The corner of her mouth tilted up. "If Bela stood, I'd be queen. Maybe that means there's still time for reconciliation."

The queen's answering smile was warm.

"But not while your son keeps my people in his dungeons."

Her smile fell. "Alexandre is his father's son, but I have hope for him yet."

Etta kept quiet, but her hope for Alex was the only thing that kept her from leaving right then to go search for a way to break the curse.

Another question entered Etta's mind and her eyes flicked to Tyson. "How did he come to have magic?"

Catrine closed her eyes briefly, tears coming once again, and ran her fingers through her son's hair. "Tyson is not a Durand. Many years ago, I fell into love with a man who could only give me my boy in return." She opened her eyes. "But it was as if he gave me the whole world."

She'd had a lover. Enough to have her executed if the king so chose. Etta found herself suppressing a smile, glad the queen found some bit of happiness.

"Now that we all know enough to get each other killed." Catrine gave her a pointed look. "The reason for coming. I need to get Tyson out of the palace."

Tyson uttered a grunt of protest, but his mother pinched him. They'd obviously already discussed what was necessary.

Etta waited for more explanation.

"With the Edmund situation, it's best he be sent into hiding."

A pang of sympathy squeezed Etta's chest, but she didn't disagree. She nodded slowly. "I take it you already have a plan?"

"He will go to the estate of Duchess Moreau."

"Is that wise?"

"Yes. She is a dear friend and has many descendants of Bela living on her land under her protection. She has offered Tyson a place for the time being."

"Then what do you need me for?" Etta cocked her head.

"You're the only person I trust to get him there safely."

She understood now. She was to be the escort. But that wasn't possible. "I'm not supposed to leave the king."

"Alexandre will be given a temporary replacement. He doesn't think he can trust any of his people after Edmund's arrest. So, I will convince him he needs to send the person he trusts most to the border for a report on La Dame's movements."

"Are you sure he'll send me?"

Catrine put a hand on Etta's shoulder. "My dear, Alexandre is in love with you, what greater trust is there than that?"

Etta shook her head violently. "All he's feeling is the curse bringing us together."

The queen stood and looked down at her as she straightened out the pleats of her dress. "Then where are the stories of your cursed ancestors falling in love with their charges?"

Etta's fingers shook, and she reached for the wine again. The pitcher slipped from her grasp, crashing to the floor. Red wine spread quickly across the stone.

"Shit." Realizing what she'd said and who she was with, Etta's face reddened. "Sorry."

"Oh dear." Catrine laughed. "Don't apologize. This whole curse business is about as twisted as they come."

Etta nodded her agreement.

Tyson bent over the spilled wine. The red liquid began to retract and return to the pitcher.

Catrine clutched her chest. "I am never going to get used to that."

"No shit." Tyson grinned.

Catrine cuffed him on the back of the head. "Language, boy."

CHAPTER 20

What changes in a palace after the king's most loyal friend is arrested? Nothing apparently. Business as usual.

When Etta dragged herself from bed after only a few hours of sleep, she swiftly dressed and twisted her hair into a braid before walking the short distance to the king's room.

She didn't know what she expected to find. He'd still been devastated when they parted the night before. After the revelations in the night with the queen and Prince Tyson, or not prince as the case may be, everything else felt so far away. There'd been only her past and her family's history on her mind.

Now the king was front and center in her head, where he belonged. She hated the thought of leaving him, especially when he was so hurt. She didn't trust anyone else to protect him. That was her job. It would hurt to be away from him, physically and mentally. She hadn't had to go through that since the curse kicked in, but she'd suffer it to protect Tyson. He was one of her people.

A guard at the king's door pushed it open for her and she was shocked to find Alex sitting on the end of his bed, pulling on his boots. He looked up when she entered, his expression bland.

"Protector," he said, standing up and squaring his shoulders. "Thank you for joining me."

She narrowed her eyes, confused. "My pleasure, your Majesty."

He gave her one short nod and grabbed his crown from the table. As he placed it on his head, Etta couldn't help the thought that it was so very odd. He never wore his crown unless he was sitting on his throne addressing his people or leaving the palace. She thought about today's schedule, realizing she didn't actually know it. There'd be a lot to do, considering it was only a day after the attack.

Alex began walking, and she fell in step behind him.

"What's first on the agenda today, your Majesty?" she asked.

His tone was neutral as he responded without looking at her. "We have a meeting with many of the nobles of Gaule. Then a private meeting with Lord Leroy. I had hoped Duchess Moreau would attend, but she has returned home to deal with a border skirmish. Then lunch ,with my mother. She's been begging for that. This afternoon is a series of meetings on the next steps to safeguard Gaule from magic folk."

"You mean from La Dame."

"Yes, that too."

Etta glanced at him skeptically, but kept her worries to herself. She knew what the nobles would want him to do. Most of them wanted the magic folk gone from their lands and they had considerable power over the king. What would he do while she wasn't there? Would she return to another purge?

Trying to have more faith in Alex than that, she pushed the thought from her mind. He was not his father.

They hurried down the hall, neither of them saying anything more. Alex seemed ... detached. Some would say he looked kingly, but that wasn't the sort of king she hoped he'd be.

The morning meetings went about as well as could be expected. There was a lot of yelling from scared nobles. They should've been terrified. Their towns could be destroyed as easily as the village yesterday. They said the crown wasn't doing enough to protect them. Alex met their accusations with a cool aloofness.

When they left, the nobles were still fighting among themselves. Etta put a hand on Alex's arm and pulled him into another hall for privacy. He stopped moving but didn't look at her.

"Alex," she said, squeezing his arm tighter.

He finally met her stare, and she searched his eyes for something, anything to tell her what was going on in his head. There was nothing but blue iciness.

"Are you okay?" she finally asked.

A flash of the man she knew entered his eyes, and he leaned forward, his voice low. "Someone once told me that if I asked that, they'd break my pretty face."

She smiled. He was there, down past the stoic king. "Are you going to break my face, then? Because I won't stop asking until I get an answer."

His expression closed off once again. "Leave it alone, Etta."

He shook his arm out of her grasp and stepped around her. Lord Leroy appeared in a rush, gasping for breath. He heaved, placing a hand on the wall.

"My lord?" Etta asked.

"Your Majesty." Lord Leroy found his voice and turned his eyes to his king. "I've been looking for you."

"We were on our way to meet you," Alex responded.

Lord Leroy smiled, and a chill raced up Etta's spine. "We found them. Lots of them."

"Magic folk?" Alex asked eagerly.

"They've been living in the Black Forest this whole time."

Etta's pulse spiked. Her father protected those people with his wards until his death. Her neighbors. Trying her best to conceal the panic on her face, she coughed. Alex paid her no mind. Instead, he watched Lord Leroy's excitement with something akin to resignation.

He lifted his shoulders in a shrug. "Okay. Send out the royal guard."

Etta opened her mouth to speak, but no words came out. The people of the forest were not the magic folk attacking villages and hurting people. They couldn't be, but in Gaule, all magic folk were treated the same. They'd be judged by the worst of them and she couldn't do a damn thing about it. She clamped her mouth shut and made a silent promise to her people that she'd find a way to help them. She had to.

Magic. It affected everything in Gaule. It controlled their fear and their strength. Alex didn't understand it. He didn't trust it.

His mother was speaking, so he turned to face her. "What?"

"Who do you trust most in this palace?" she asked again.

"What kind of question is that?"

"The kind I'd like you to answer."

He didn't have to think twice about who he trusted most. Other than his mother, it was Etta. Only Etta. His sworn sword. His lover. His ... well, he wasn't sure what she was.

He'd been walking around all day in a fog. Yes, your Majesty. No, your Majesty. No one questioned him. He was king. His wishes were law. So, why was Edmund still in the dungeon? Because of magic.

Instead of answering her, a growl sounded low in his throat. "I don't know why you're asking me this."

A hand landed on his arm and he looked down to stare at her long fingers, unable to meet her eyes. "Because, my son, you know as well as I that things have changed. Loyalties cannot be trusted. We don't know who our enemies are and who our friends are. And someone must go do a survey of La Dame's movements, inspect the wall surround Dracon. See how much time we have."

He finally looked at her face, trying to read what she wasn't saying.

“That isn’t a one-person mission,” he said.

His mother cocked her head. “It is if you’re trying to mask the true objective.”

Understanding struck him. She was making a plea for a man she also thought of as her son. She was giving him a way out of the dark place he’d been stuck in. A lifeline.

He leaned back with a sigh. She was right. They didn't have any more time to waste. He knew who he'd have to send, and the truth twisted in his gut. She wasn't supposed to leave his side, but he had no other choice.

"Etta," he said. "It has to be Etta."

A smile he didn't understand appeared on his mother's lips. "You trust her?"

With my life, he wanted to say. Instead, he just issued a short nod. Before, he wouldn't have hesitated to send Edmund.

Alex pushed back his chair and stood, suddenly unable to even look at the food in front of him. He'd sent Etta into the outer castle to procure a new bow as his had been lost in the attack. In truth, he'd needed some breathing room.

As he walked from the hall, he called to his page who'd been waiting for him outside the doors. "Cancel my afternoon."

There was no need for kings to explain and he brushed past the page on his way toward the cold stairwell. Emptiness had replaced his anger, and he was prepared to face his once-friend again, ready for answers.

Edmund didn't look at him when he entered the dank room. Taking the keys he'd gotten from the guards, he unlocked the door to the cell, knowing Edmund's chains kept him in place.

"Are you afraid I'm going to harm you?" Edmund snapped his eyes to the king and the coldness in them made Alex stop.

"You have magic, Edmund." Alex folded his arms. "I don't think the bars of your cell would stop you from harming me."

Edmund's expression thawed before his cool mask shifted back into place. "Here to give me my execution date, your Majesty?"

Alex began to pace the cell. "I'm so angry, Edmund."

"Clearly."

"Don't do that. Don't treat me like we don't know each other at all."

"I'm not the one locking friends in the dungeon."

"What would you have me do?" Alex yelled, running a hand through his hair, knocking the crown off his head. It clattered to the ground at Edmund's feet. "I am the king, Edmund. In Gaule, it's illegal to have magic."

"How can I be a criminal for something I didn't choose?"

Alex stopped moving and sat down, not caring how filthy the ground was. His shoulders sagged, and all power left his voice. "I don't know." He looked up into the eyes of his friend, eyes that were no longer cold as they flooded with sympathy. "Do you remember the first day we met?"

Edmund's lips tugged into a smile and he nodded.

"You told me everything there was to know about you in a single conversation." He looked away. "Everything except this."

"You'd have arrested me on the spot."

"The irony is that back then I probably wouldn't have."

"Why did you come down here today?" Edmund asked; his chains rattling as he shifted.

Alex rubbed the back of his neck. "I ... I didn't want last night to be the last time I saw you." He paused. "I ..." He closed his mouth, deciding against the words he was going to say.

"So, I am to be executed, then." Edmund’s voice shook as he spoke.

Alex got to his feet and snatched his crown off the floor as he walked past the bars. While locking the cell once again, he looked down at his friend. "No, Edmund." He ran a hand through his hair, pulling on the ends. “No … you knew I’d do this.”

“Do what?”

“Risk everything to save you. If the nobles find out…”

The hope that sprang into Edmund's eyes was too much for Alex. He turned away to walk back down the long hall. Before his feet began to move, Edmund spoke at his back, his words almost too quiet to hear.

"I love you, Alex. If I'm never going to see you again, to look into your eyes, then I guess this is the time for confessions." He laughed softly. "I think I've loved you since that first day when you asked me to just be your friend."

Alex closed his eyes. He'd known. He'd always known.

"I love you, too." It wasn't the same. Alex knew it. Edmund knew it. Alex's love was that of a friend, a brother. But it was powerful all the same.

As he walked away, two words floated on the air behind him.

"Thank you."

CHAPTER 21

Etta felt eyes on her as she made her way back to the palace; bow firmly clutched in her hand. She didn't understand why Alex was so attached to the thing. She'd only ever used them for hunting. For fighting, a bow and arrow were no good. She'd rather be in the middle of the fray rather than taking down enemies from afar.

She wondered if her father would tell her she'd lost her objective, entrenching herself so far into the Durand household. But that was her job, wasn't it?

Someone moved in an alley to her left and she suddenly wished she had arrows to go with the bow. She walked closer to the alley, leaning the bow against the side of the building to free her hands. She opted to draw her dagger instead of her sword.

As she rounded the side of the shop, someone moved and she spun to launch a kick right into their stomach. They let out a squeal and sagged against the building. Grabbing the person's arm, she twisted and brought up her dagger. Breathing heavily, her eyes began to clear from the haze of fighting. Chocolate curls swam in her vision.

"Maiya?" She released the girl and shoved her knife into its sheath along her leg. "I'm so sorry."

Maiya bent over, holding her stomach, wheezing. "It's okay, Etta. Everyone's a bit jumpy these days."

Etta examined her friend from head to toe. She was real. She was alive. She was there, within the castle. Before Etta knew what she was doing, she'd pulled the smaller girl into a crushing hug.

"Were you following me?" Etta asked, releasing her.

"No. I only spotted you moments before you attacked me."

"I did not attack you."

Maiya laughed. "Then what would you call that?"

Etta huffed. "I've been so worried about you. I didn't know if you'd made it out of the village or if ..."

Maiya grabbed her arms. "Look at me. I'm fine."

Etta examined her again and released a sigh. "You are."

"I've been trying to find a way to contact you, but they aren't letting anyone past the inner gates."

"It's too dangerous for us to be seen together, you know that."

"I do, but ..." Tears shone in Maiya's amber eyes.

"But what?"

"They have my father."

Etta closed her eyes for a brief moment. She knew exactly who "they" were. Alex's men. Pierre was in the dungeons.

"Tell me everything."

Maiya did. Standing in that alley, she talked of watching the fight rage along the street in front of her shop. She thought they were goners. Then Etta and Alex escaped, leaving Edmund to fight all on his own. Pierre joined him in an attempt to save a handful of families who were being terrorized. The guards saw them both and when the fight was over, they took them to the dungeons.

"Etta, you have to get him out of there," Maiya pleaded.

"How am I supposed to do that?"

"Talk to the king."

Etta met the other girl's unblinking stare. "The king won't even help his friend." Etta was surprised at the resentment in her own voice. Maybe Alex was the man she'd thought he was all along—his father's son.

"Please."

"Maiya, I can't plead for every magic man's life, especially when the only thing it will do is cast suspicion onto me."

"You won't even try?"

"I'm sorry."

Maiya backed away from her, shaking her head as tears coursed down her dark skin. Without another word, she turned and ran down the alley, disappearing around the corner.

Pierre weighed on Etta's mind as she picked up the bow and made her way back to the palace.

The king was in the garden with Lord Leroy when she approached.

Lord Leroy saw her and took his leave. Alex barely noticed her as something foreboding brewed in his eyes.

When will it end? Etta thought, looking at him. *This battle. This heartbreak.*

The rest of the day passed in a blur. Even after clearing his schedule, nobles and advisers insisted on meeting with the king. Alex only spoke when he had to. He refused to meet Etta's eyes and shrank away from her touch. So, she stopped trying, very aware that if he knew the real Etta, he'd hate her just as much as he now hated Edmund. And that thought stole the breath from her lungs.

She was supposed to hate the King of Gaule. Now she couldn't stand the thought of any ill will towards him.

Etta sank into her bed that night feeling weary and confused. The night she first took up the curse, her soul fractured from the weight of it. Now those cracks were widening with each passing day. Soon, the fragments would no longer fit together and that was when the curse would win. When La Dame could claim her victory. When she would destroy the newest in a long line of Basiles.

Persinette would become the newest in the long line of Basiles to descend into the dark pits of pain and despair.

Alex's mind was not on any of his kingly duties as days turned into nights. The soldiers brought people in from the Black Forest almost daily now. The dungeons were nearly filled to capacity. No one had realized so many magic folk still remained in Gaule.

Most thought it was the work of Viktor Basile, keeping them hidden. That man saved countless lives, but they were people who shouldn't have been in Gaule at all. The purge was meant to exterminate them.

A shiver ran up Alex's spine.

Edmund was still a prisoner, but Alex had made up his mind. He'd chosen the kind of king he wanted to be. He just needed a little help.

Running his hand over the smooth wood of his bow, he marveled at the simplicity of such a weapon. How could something made simply of wood and string kill a man? How could it pierce armor or feed a family?

Shooting calmed him. It allowed his mind to go blank. He lined up his shot, raising his elbow, and breathing in as his finger pulled the string taut. As he exhaled, he sent the arrow flying toward the target. It hit the center with a thud.

He knew his guards mocked him when they thought he wasn't watching because of his lack of skill with a sword. They thought it made him less of a man. Less of a warrior. Who wanted a king that wasn't a warrior? His father had been able to best almost every man in his guard.

Except for Edmund.

A smile curved Alex's mouth. The day Edmund beat his father in a duel had been one of the greatest days he could remember. Alex's father punished Edmund for the embarrassment by making him work in the kitchens during the evening meal. Alex helped him and thought nothing could be more worth it.

Alex stepped in front of a new target, this one a farther distance. The arrow sailed just as true as the first, landing exactly where the king planned. He laughed to himself, feeling at ease for the first time in days. This, he was good at. This, he could do. Unlike being king.

He didn't know what he was doing. For the first time since his father was killed, he wished he were still here. Not out of any sense of love—he knew what the man had been—but because Alex didn't think he was strong enough to lead his people against La Dame, or any of the other magic folk for that matter.

His finger shook as he drew back the string again. This time when he fired, the arrow wobbled in the air before arcing toward the ground, just short of the target. Like him, it hadn't had the power to do what was necessary.

How could he fight magic while considering what he'd been thinking about doing? Did it make him a hypocrite or worse, a traitor to go through with his plan?

"Brother."

Alex sighed as his sister's voice permeated his sanctuary. He'd been alone for the past hour, the guards giving him the practice yard to himself. Camille didn't exercise the same courtesy.

He lowered his bow and turned slowly. "Camille."

She looked to the ground as if trying to force vulnerability into her face. But Alex knew his sister. Behind her mask of fragile porcelain skin, was steel, cold and uncaring. He hadn't seen much of her in the time since their father's death. She'd been in mourning for the one man who didn't see her for the heartless princess she was. Or maybe he did, but he would have enjoyed that quality in a daughter.

Her voice was meek when she spoke, but she wasn't fooling him. "I have come to see what you plan to do with the traitor, Edmund."

"I don't see how that concerns you," he snapped.

"Of course it does. It concerns all of Gaule. Your punishment will set a precedent. There should be no special treatment. All magic should be treated equally."

Alex turned away from her to face the target once again. "Leave me, Camille."

"Not until you realize that you are king of Gaule. Not Dracon. Not Bela. The people of Gaule are the ones counting on you to erase the scourge in our lands. To keep us safe." She put her hands on her hips. "Anders and I have been discussing it. If you cannot sentence Edmund, as you should, we can take care of the problem for you. Discretely, of course."

Alex barely spared a moment to think before charging at her. She at least had the decency to appear afraid as his hands closed around her upper arms and he bent to force her to look into his eyes.

"If you touch one hair on his head, Camille, I swear ..."

"You'll what?" She pushed him away, and he dropped his arms. "He isn't your brother, Alexandre. But I am your sister. Maybe it's time you re-examine where your true loyalty lies." She narrowed her eyes, preparing to land the killing blow. "The guard in the dungeons tells me we have more than one reason to sentence him harshly."

"Spit it out."

"A confession he made to you today. The guard heard everything. He will serve as witness." She stepped closer and dropped her voice dangerously. "Loving another man is punishable by death, here in Gaule. Even if the man you're screwing is the king."

Alex's hand flew through the air, striking Camille's cheek with more force than he'd intended. The edge of her lip burst open and as she stuck out her tongue to test the cut, they stood in stunned silence.

Alex gripped her chin so hard he was surprised she still hadn't made a sound.

"Sister, I'd watch your tongue before I have it cut out. I am still your king and I'd rather have Edmund by my side than a twisted princess." He released her with a jerk and her head snapped back.

When she pinned him with her eyes again, hatred swirled in their depths.

"You are dismissed," Alex growled.

She picked up the hem of her long skirt and limped from his presence, her curses ringing in the night air.

Alex ran a hand through his hair and released a long breath, feeling somewhat better about what he had to do. He wasn't betraying everything Gaule stood for. He was preventing himself from becoming like his sister.

"Don't do it." The voice came from behind him and he turned to see Tyson. His brother must have heard the entire conversation and his eyes shone as he hurried forward in complete contrast to their sister. "Alex, please. It's Edmund. I don't care what Camille says or if he has magic. I don't care who Edmund loves. Wouldn't you rather keep someone around who is loyal to you out of love rather than duty? You can't execute him, and you can't keep him in those dungeons either."

"Tyson." Alex put a hand on his brother's shoulder. "No one is being executed."

"Really? Because they've been building gallows outside the walls."

Alex cursed. Safety reasons kept him from traveling past the inner walls to discover what his captain had been doing. He didn't want to lie to his brother. There'd be people calling for the heads of every magic man or woman they captured. The only thing he could tell Tyson for certain was that Edmund wouldn't be one of them. Alex had a plan.

"I'll take care of it, Ty."

Tyson scrutinized Alex, unconvinced. Alex gripped his shoulder and pulled him into a hug, thumping his back roughly. "It's going to be okay."

Neither of them believed the words, but they felt good to say anyway.

CHAPTER 22

Etta paced the hall outside Tyson's door. They should have left already. Tyson needed to be out of the palace before his secrets were revealed. Days. Etta had been waiting for days for Alex to bring up a mission to the border. Surely the queen would have succeeded in convincing him.

What the hell was taking him so long?

She'd been kicked out of a meeting. She was supposed to stand at the king's side for all things, but Anders blocked her as she'd tried to enter. He had a need to speak with the king alone. The distrust was evident in his eyes. When Alex assured her he'd be safe with his captain, she didn't argue.

She was so damn tired of the secrets; the hatred pointed her way.

Just like days ago when she'd walked through the outer palace, she felt eyes watching her every move as she removed her sword belt and set it on the long wooden table to the side of the practice yard. She spun to find Princess Camille glaring at her from the steps.

Trying to ignore the harsh stare, Etta ran a hand over the knives before her, choosing one at random. She spun again, and with a flick of her hand sent the knife flying end over end, watching as it sank into the farthest target. She looked back just quickly enough to see the princess flinch.

Etta smirked and picked up another knife, balancing it in her palm. She took her time weighing it, considering its direction. When she released it this time, she used her full arm to gain momentum; throwing the knife with such force its impact rang throughout the yard.

Etta threw the remaining two knives before walking forward to retrieve them. When she turned back, she realized she had an audience. Men and women in guard's uniforms paused their training to watch the enigmatic king's protector. The girl who'd bested and killed some of their comrades in the tournament.

Etta never had much to do with the guards. They were as mysterious to her as she was to them. As she scanned the curious faces, she couldn't help but wonder who among them had been sent into the Black Forest to find her people. Who'd arrested Edmund? Were the older guards around when her father had been hunted?

Her lungs tried to expand, but she couldn't breathe. Despite the friendly looks sent her way, these people weren't her friends.

Enemies, she thought. *I'm surrounded by enemies.*

She lurched toward the table and slammed the knives down so hard it shook.

They parted for her as she ran through the crowd, panic building in her chest. Camille was gone by the time Etta's feet thundered up the steps. She didn't stop until she'd reached her room and slammed the door behind her. She leaned back against it, breathing heavily.

She had to get out. Why wasn't she gone?

Tonight, she had to find Queen Catrine. Something was wrong.

She slid down the door until her butt hit the floor, sending a shockwave up her spine. Her breath returned to normal, and she wiped the sweat from her hair.

After a few minutes, she climbed to her feet and made her way to the washbasin. She splashed lukewarm water on her face and over the top of her hair. It ran down her scalp, soaking into her shirt.

She'd have to meet the king after his meeting, but she couldn't make herself go back out that door.

Pulling the damp shirt over her head, she found a dry one and laid back on her bed to get her muscles to loosen. She'd just stay there for a moment and then she'd go to the king. Just a moment.

After hours of listening to Anders go on about his plan for dealing with the magic folk, Alex left to find Etta, to apologize. Anders had no right to treat her so poorly, and she'd had every right as protector to be in that meeting.

But what was he to say to her? They'd been acting like nothing more than a king and his subject since returning from the forest, since that night. Did he have to apologize for that too?

Etta wasn't in the practice yard, nor the hall. As he was looking, he was pulled away by Lord Leroy and then it was time for dinner. His mother thought he needed to eat in the hall with his men. Show them his confidence; that he believed in them and in Gaule.

Dinner lasted into the evening with his men drinking and telling stories. Some of them reminded him of Edmund and then guilt stabbed at him every time he laughed.

The wine buzzed in his veins, but his head was still clear.

One of the older officers stood up to make a toast and raised his glass. "To the king." The men cheered. "To Gaule. To destroying magic within our borders once and for all." He looked to Alex. "I am sure his majesty agrees that we must begin upholding the laws of Gaule. The gallows are finished, although a hanging is more humane than these animals deserve." A rumble of agreement made its way around the room. "I say we start with the man who pretended to be one of us."

Alex's heart stopped as he heard what the men were asking for.

Someone else yelled to be heard. "Two days and then we can kill the bastard on the anniversary of the day the great purge began!"

Alex struggled to keep a calm expression as everything in him ripped to pieces. If he pardoned Edmund now, they'd call him a sympathizer. He'd lose support. His eyes found Anders and the man's expression hadn't changed with the calls for his son's death.

Didn't his son mean anything to him?

There could be no further delay. Unless he wanted to watch Edmund dangle by his neck, he had to do something.

He pounded his fist against the table to capture the attention of the room. Once. Twice.

They quieted and turned to look at him. He stood and pushed his chair back. They waited for him to say something important, kingly. "I must retire." As he walked away, he heard their confused whispers follow him from the hall.

His personal guards followed him and when he reached Etta's door, his scowl sent them scurrying away.

She couldn't avoid him forever.

He closed his eyes. Despite the distance growing between them, he'd missed her.

But this visit was not about him.

He raised his fist and pounded on Etta's door. No one answered, so he did it again.

After what seemed like an eternity, the door opened and Etta stood before him with sleep-clouded eyes and her golden hair hanging wildly about her face.

Alex sucked in a breath. She was the most exquisite thing he'd ever seen. The invisible tug inside him that he'd been trying to ignore for days, pulled him in closer, until he could smell her sweet scent. She rubbed her face and considered him with guarded eyes.

"I'm sorry, your Majesty," she said. "I ... fell asleep." She stepped back away from him, an invitation to enter the room.

He slammed the door behind him, wanting nothing more than to take her into his arms. But he couldn't. This was too important.

"Etta," he rasped. "I need you to do something. It's important and you can't tell anyone."

Relief flooded her features, and he didn't understand why.

"Of course," she said softly.

"Officially, I'm going to send you to the border where you'll meet up with a contingent of Duchess Moreau's soldiers to see what you can find out about La Dame's movements."

"And unofficially?"

"You're taking Edmund to the border." Once the words were out, there was no taking them back. If he wasn't king, this would be treason.

If Etta were caught, she'd be charged.

A smile appeared on her face, transforming quickly into a full-blown grin. She stepped closer. "We're getting him out?"

He nodded.

"When do I leave?"

"As soon as possible." He pulled a set of keys from his pocket and set it on the table. "That will get him out."

"I'll leave in the morning."

A weight lifted from his chest, but it was soon replaced with a new one. Worry? He shook the thought from his mind as he watched Etta continue to grin at him. As if moving of its own accord, his arm lifted. He had to touch her. His fingers brushed along the curved line of her lower lip.

"I like that I finally did something to make you smile again," he said.

She closed her eyes, leaning into his touch. "I'm just glad my king is doing the right thing."

"Your king. Is that all I am to you?"

Her eyes snapped open, and he was lost in their intensity.

"No. You're my Alex. Still the boy I've always loved."

He raised his brow in confusion, but that was pushed aside with the new realization that he was so irrevocably in love. It didn't matter that she was a commoner or that her hands had been bathed in blood. She was his.

His hand slid around to the back of her neck and he pulled her to him. She came willingly, her mouth inviting him to fall deeper. She kissed him with all of the softness he hadn't known she possessed. His lips moved slowly over hers and when her tongue met his, a growl sounded low in his throat. He pulled her closer, their bodies flush, needing to touch her in every way he could.

His hands inched up beneath her shirt and over the warm skin of her back. She sighed as his fingers traced the curve of her spine. They broke apart and stared for a moment before removing their shirts. Etta placed a palm against Alex's bare chest.

"I still don't know if this is real, but even if we only have this moment, I want it more than I've ever wanted anything." Sorrow filled her gaze, and he wanted to wipe it away but he let her continue speaking. "Whatever happens, Alex, you have to know that I love you."

He took her hand and brought it to his lips. "What's going to happen?"

She looked down, uncertainty written across her posture. His chest ached to see the confident Etta in such a state. He put his fingers under her chin and tilted her face up to look at him. "Nothing is going to tear us apart."

She reached for him, wrapping her arms around his neck as she pressed her chest against his and kissed him like it was the last thing she'd ever do. Her words vibrated against his lips. "I wish that were true."

“It is. You’ll get Edmund to safety and then return to me. I’ll break off my betrothal. For you. I want you, everything you have to give, everything you are.”

Her breath shuddered as she wrapped her legs around his waist and let him carry her to the bed. They never lost contact as they removed the rest of their clothes.

It was different from their night in the Black Forest. Etta was different. Desperation charged the air as she moved over him with every ounce of power and need she held. When he flipped her over to worship her in the way she deserved, she held him close, never wanting to let go.

As they drifted off to sleep that night, Alex held her tightly. She laid her head on his chest as their legs tangled together.

He closed his eyes as her breath evened out.

He didn't know if her final words were from her mouth or a dream.

"You're not the man I thought you'd be. You're a good man, Alexandre Durand. But good men aren't meant to be kings." She pressed her lips to his forehead. "I wasn't supposed to fall in love with you."

When he woke in the morning, she was gone.

CHAPTER 23

She wasn't coming back. The realization had struck her the moment she told Alex how she'd felt the night before. If she was to take Edmund and Tyson to Duchess Moreau near the border, she'd cross it and make the journey into Dracon. That's where La Dame would be.

It was the only way.

She couldn't go on loving him when it might not be real. The truth was precious and must be found. If she still loved him when they were no longer tied, she'd find him.

But she knew that wouldn't happen.

Kissing him goodbye in the middle of the night had nearly broken her heart, and she'd barely registered where she was going until her feet stopped outside Queen Catrine's door. The queen pulled her in and scanned for other onlookers. Seeing a deserted corridor, she came back into the room.

Catrine had been preparing for days, not knowing when they'd leave, and everything was ready.

Before Etta could explain her presence, Catrine was on the move. "I'll wake Tyson."

Nerves battled in Etta's chest as she waited. She hadn't wanted to leave Alex sleeping. They deserved a better ending than that.

Her feet scuffed along the floor as she paced. This was her chance. She didn't know if she could break the curse, but she had to try.

It was time to see La Dame. Would the sorceress speak to her? Maybe she'd kill her on the spot. But if there was even the slightest chance she was the key to breaking the curse, Etta had to take it. It was the only piece of the puzzle she knew.

Closing her eyes, she pictured Alex back in her room, his face relaxed in sleep. He'd never forgive her for this.

The real question was about what happened after. Once the curse no longer tied her to this place, where would she go then?

Before she could dwell on too many what ifs, Tyson stumbled into the room, pulling on a shirt. His head popped through the hole with his dark hair flopping into his eyes. He looked so much like his brother, but there was something about him that was also very different. Knowing the dead king was not his father solved many riddles.

He shot her a nervous smile. "Hey, Persinette."

Her shoulders dropped. "We should probably stick with Etta for the time being."

He nodded, but didn't say anything more. The usually energetic, talkative prince was gone, replaced by this nervous boy who looked even younger than his years.

"We should head out. We need to get to Edmund."

That perked him up, and he blew out a puff of air, clearly relieved. "Alex?"

"The king wants us to get Edmund out of Gaule."

"I knew he'd never let anything happen to Edmund."

Queen Catrine walked up, handing each of them a pack stuffed with food for the journey. Etta stiffened when she pulled her into her arms.

"Be safe, Persinette," she whispered.

Etta rested her chin on the queen's shoulder. "Take care of him."

"Same goes to you." She released Etta and gestured to Tyson.

"I will. With my life."

"I know." The queen smiled. "You've always been a warrior, Etta. Even when you were just a girl running along the walls or climbing towers to entertain my son." Her smiled tightened. "I hope there comes a day when you won't have to fight anymore."

The words sank into Etta and she turned away. The day she no longer had to fight would be the day she had nothing. Her hand grazed the hilt of her sword. Sometimes it was the only thing that made sense.

She moved to the door as the queen said a tearful goodbye to her son. He bowed his head as his mother kissed it and then pushed him toward the door.

Etta peered into the hall. When she didn't see anyone, she hiked the bag up on her shoulder and started to run. Tyson followed her, and she craned her neck to see around the corner. The palace halls were abandoned, making it an easy trek to the dungeons.

The two guards could be heard at the bottom of the stairs.

"Stay here, Tyson," she whispered. Her sword scraped as she drew it slowly and inched down the stairwell into the dark. The steps were illuminated by small lanterns hanging on the wall.

Her steps were light, and she managed to make it to the bottom without a sound.

The guards were standing in front of one of the cells, laughing about the poor soul inside. Rage boiled up inside her and she wanted to gut them right then.

No. No more killing.

She released a growl as she burst from the stairwell in a speed of fury. The guards turned but weren't quick enough. She lunged at the first, knocking him out with a swift rap of her hilt. The second came at her from behind, wrapping his arms around her waist. She lunged back, slamming him into the wall. One arm remained around her wrist while the other tried to cut off her air supply, closing tightly around her throat. She gasped and kicked as a knifepoint dug into her back.

Slamming her head back into his nose, she broke his hold and spun with her sword in hand. Dark blood ran from his nose.

"You're asking for it, bitch," he growled.

Etta bent her knees, preparing for his attack. When he finally came at her, it was a slow and feeble attempt. She flung out her arm and sliced her sword through his side. He fell back against the wall and slid down. She waited for him to make another move, but it never came. So much for no killing.

After wiping her blade on the man's shirt, she sheathed it and headed into the darkness among the cheers from prisoner's who caught her fight.

The queen's words came back to her. What would she do if she weren't fighting? That was what she was good at. She kept going until she turned and stopped outside Edmund's cell.

He lay on the ground, unmoving. His facial hair had grown, adding to his raggedy look. His blond mop was matted and streaked with dirt. A bruise faded along his jawline. He didn't look like he'd been touched since—probably on Alex's orders.

She pulled the key out of her pocket and fumbled with the lock before stumbling through and falling to her knees at Edmund's side.

"Edmund," she whispered, reaching out tentatively to grab his shoulder and shake it. "Wake up." He was so still she'd worry he was dead if not for the pulse beating in his neck. "Come on."

His crusty eyes fluttered open, and he moved his mouth as if to speak. No words came.

"I'm getting you out of here," she whispered. "Alex wants you safe. Come on, I have water just up the steps."

She pulled on his arm and he finally gathered the strength to push himself slowly to his feet. Etta draped his arm over her shoulders and they made it back to the stairs and past the two guards she'd fought. It took quite a bit more time for them to reach Tyson at the top.

His anxious face greeted them. "Etta, someone heard the fight. They've sounded the alarm."

CHAPTER 24

Boots crashed against stone with a loud rhythm as guards ran throughout the palace, roused from their sleep by the bell ringing overhead.

Tyson helped Edmund stay on his feet as the three of them waited, hidden in the darkness of an unused hallway. They'd look there soon enough. The entire palace would be scoured for the escaped prisoner. Then the search would spill out into the outer castle. The king couldn't stop it.

They needed to be gone by then.

Etta knew where they needed to go and her heart kicked into overdrive. She hadn't been there since the night she and her father escaped all those years ago, but there was no way they were getting past the inner gates. Not with Edmund slung between them as if screaming, "It's me! Arrest me again!"

Etta blew out a breath and studied the broken man and the prince beside him. What was she doing?

Shaking her head, she looked away. "Helping you two is going to get me killed. Come on."

They slipped out a little-known door at the end of the hall. Like Tyson, Etta spent her younger years sneaking around the palace, usually chasing Alex, and finding new ways to get into trouble in the outer castle. She knew where she was going.

As they skirted the courtyard, hidden in the shadows, Etta paused. Alex walked down the steps, still rubbing his face from sleep.

Three guards ran up to him. Alex's eyes scanned the courtyard, widening when he saw them crouching near the entrance. One of his guards turned to see what had caught the king's attention, and another entered, stopping right in front of Etta.

"Soldier," Alex barked.

Both guards snapped to attention.

"Report."

"Sire, they aren't in the palace. My men are being sent past the inner gates. I'll send someone to check the stables to see if they've taken horses, and the others will begin a house by house search."

Alex's face hardened. "I've sent someone to the stables already. Commence with the search. Someone must be hiding them."

They bowed and ran past him to give their orders. Alex stayed in place for a moment longer. His eyes burned into Etta. He gave a single nod of his head and turned to go back inside.

There was no time to dwell on goodbyes. Etta led Tyson and Edmund from the courtyard.

"He just cleared the stables for us," she whispered. "But we still have to get there."

Their destination wasn't far. It was the only place that could take them into the outer castle without passing the gates. The house was the same. It was a two-room shanty squished up against the wall as if it never really belonged there. The thatched roof sat in need of repair, but there was a glowing candle in the window, signaling the fact it had new owners. Owners who weren't her parents. They'd been untroubled there. At least, that's what her child eyes had seen. Now she wondered if anyone could truly be content when they were cursed. Had her father pretended during all the years they lived within those walls?

"When I was little," Etta began, looking at Tyson out of the corner of her eye. "I had a penchant for thievery. It got me in a lot of trouble with my father, but I discovered how to get in and out of the outer castle so I stayed off the king's radar." She smiled at the memory. "Although, your brother was usually egging me on."

Edmund made a sound deep in his throat, but there was no time to explain. Honesty would come later.

She ran on silent feet to the side of the house. The crates they'd kept their chickens in were still there. She turned back to the boys. "Okay, we need to try this as quietly as possible. There are people sleeping in there."

The sound of a door opening, made her spin, coming face to face with a small girl with wide eyes. She tugged on her blond hair and stared.

Etta held her breath, waiting for the girl to scream or cry or do something to wake her parents.

Tyson moved forward. "It's okay, I'm the prince."

She hesitated and stepped back.

"Please don't wake your parents," Etta said.

The girl finally spoke. "Momma and Daddy went in to work when the alarm sounded. They're guards."

Etta didn't waste any time. "Tyson, we have to go." She climbed the crates that no longer held chickens and jumped like she'd done a thousand times before. Her fingers gripped onto the edge of the roof and her legs dangled beneath her before she managed to pull herself up, her adult body able to do this more easily than before.

"Edmund is next." She kneeled at the edge and reached her hand down. "He won't make the jump in his state. Tyson, you'll have to hoist him and between the two of us we can get him up here."

Tyson bent, gripping Edmund's legs and strained. He was a strong teen and Edmund was lean. Edmund's reached up and she gripped his arms, using the roof as leverage to pull. By the time he was up, her chest heaved. Tyson made the jump easily.

The wall was only a step up and as they went over the top onto the smith shop's roof on the other side, Etta glanced back to see the girl still watching them.

They made it to the stables without a problem, thanks to the king. He kept the guards busy with a house to house search. The stable lad on duty for the night was asleep against the wall, and with one thump from Tyson, he wouldn't be waking to see them saddling the horses.

Vérité kicked at his stall in excitement as Etta neared. She smiled. "We're getting out of here, boy. You and me. Freedom, how does that sound? But first we'll have to go break this curse."

The horse snorted.

"I don't care if you don't believe me," she snapped, hoisting his saddle off the hook outside his stall. She ran a hand along his back. "You and me, buddy."

Once Vérité was saddled, she led him from the stall among a chorus of snorts and neighs coming from the other stalls. Tyson was waiting for her beside an all-white stallion. Edmund pushed away from the wall he'd been using to prop himself up.

"You're with me," Etta told him, gesturing to Vérité.

"You expect me to ride that thing?"

"Edmund, shut up. You know as well as I that you'd fall off if you tried to ride on your own right now." She shot him a smirk. "I promise he won't bite you."

He cursed and walked toward her. Tyson and Etta both steadied him as he got on. Etta attached the bag Catrine had given her to the saddle and stowed her sword behind it. She pulled herself up in front of Edmund and gave Vérité a kick. They thundered from the stable. Tyson followed close behind.

Guards ran out onto the street yelling, but before they could get the outer gates closed, the two horses slipped through.

Etta turned off the road to gallop across the open ground, wanting to put as much distance between them and the castle as she could.

They rode for hours with no sign of pursuit, though she was sure they were coming after them. It'd be three days of hard riding to reach Duchess Moreau's land.

Rolling fields gave way as trees enveloped them. They ducked to get under a branch and had to slow on the uneven ground.

Edmund clutched her tighter around the waist as he swayed.

"Are you okay?" she asked.

"Never better, Persinette." He bit off her name with disappointment in his voice.

Her hands held the reins so tightly her knuckles turned white. "You know."

"I should have seen it before."

"How? You didn't know me when I lived here before."

A tree stretched across the path in front of them, blocking their way. Etta lifted her hand, and the branches began to bend and shrink until there was a wide enough gap for the horses.

She barely noticed she'd used her magic until she saw Tyson's stunned face. "And I thought my water thing was cool."

Edmund jerked his eyes toward Tyson. "You have magic?"

In answer, Tyson took a seemingly empty water canister and focused on it before handing it to Edmund, water sloshing over the side.

"It seems I missed a lot." Edmund shrugged and took a long drink before handing it back to Tyson and returning to the earlier topic. "I may not have known you, Etta, but I felt like I did." He shook his head. "I met Alex the week after you and your father ran. He was a mess and talked about you ... a lot."

"He was probably just a little traumatized."

"I take it he doesn't know who you are?" he asked.

She shook her head. She hadn't wanted him to recognize her, but the fact he hadn't still hurt. She would've recognized him anywhere.

"Right." Bitterness tinged his words. "Or else you would've been in that dungeon with me."

Etta's shoulders began to shake as the truth of his words rang in her mind. Edmund nudged her.

"Hey," he said. "Alex also got me out."

"In a way that no one would know he was involved. I worry that without us there, he's going to follow in his father's footsteps."

"But you're planning to go back, right?"

As she contemplated his question, a jolt of pain shot through her. It threw her sideways as she screamed out. She fell from Vérité's back before Edmund could catch her.

A burst of wind slowed her descent, courtesy of Edmund.

Edmund and Tyson jumped from their saddles and rushed toward her as she writhed on the forest floor. Her breath came in gasps.

"Etta, what's happening?" Edmund winced as he knelt, trying not to fall over next to her.

"Is it the curse?" Tyson asked.

Edmund jerked back, his voice no more than a reverent whisper. "The Basile curse? The legends are true?" He didn't wait for an answer as he leaned forward. "That's it. Why you came back. You're tied to Alex."

She scowled up at him as the pain began to dull to a low throb. "I'm glad you're having an epiphany, because all I feel is pain."

"Everyone knows the stories of a curse that brought down an entire country, but that's all they were. Stories. Pretend."

"Well, I'm not pretending. This fucking hurts." A growl ripped from her throat as she laid back and raised her eyes to the sky. Tears pricked the edges of her lids. The farther from Alex she got, the worse it would feel. That pain was only the beginning.

He must have been feeling it too, and she was strangely glad for that. It meant she wasn't alone.

Tyson pulled her to her feet. "We're far enough from the palace now and you look like death, so we should rest for the night."

She nodded, not having the will to argue. She used her last bit of strength to create logs for the fire before curling up next to its warmth.

That night, Tyson told Edmund everything. About him. About her. Etta closed her eyes, too drained to care as her world shifted once more, the balance she'd fought so hard to keep ebbing away.

CHAPTER 25

Would the betrayals never end?

Alex stormed through the castle, nothing in his head but rage. He couldn't see the people he passed or the guards that followed at a distance. The only thing on his mind was his destination.

His fist sounded like thunder on the door to the dowager queen's suite. She let him in but didn't shrink away from his ire.

"Mother," he growled. "Tell me why I just saw Tyson accompanying Etta out of the palace?"

The queen's eyes widened as she gasped. "You didn't stop them, did you?"

He slammed the still open door and charged farther into the room. "Of course not. If I had, I'd have sent both Etta and Edmund to the hangman."

She released a breath she'd been holding, and the anger began to drain from him as he studied his mother's worried face.

"Mother, tell me what's going on. Where is my brother?"

She shook her head and backed away, fear finally entering her gaze.

"Are you afraid of me?" The question hurt him to ask.

For a moment, he thought she wasn't going to answer. She sank slowly onto the couch. "Tyson is not a Durand," his mom choked out.

Alex's first instinct was to deny her words. Of course Tyson was a Durand. He was a prince of Gaule. Beloved brother of the king.

"It's true," she said. "His father had magic."

Alex collapsed into a chair, his legs no longer able to hold him up. He hung his head as his mother's words sank in. Tyson had magic. And he'd just run because he feared what his own brother would do to him. Just like Edmund.

Everyone expected him to bring a new purge. He thought he hated magic. He'd seen the evil it could do. But he also knew Edmund and Tyson and he couldn't hate them.

And they'd believed the worst of him. He raised his tortured gaze to the queen. "Mother," he croaked.

She jumped to her feet and rushed toward him, bending to wrap him in her arms.

"I would have protected him." Alex's voice shook. "He didn't need to run from me."

"You would have tried, my sweet boy. I believe you would have tried."

"I don't know what to think anymore."

"None of us do."

She released him and he wiped at his face.

"Who is Tyson's father?"

"Someone I cared for very much, but it isn't important. He is lost to us."

"Did you love Father?"

She smiled sadly. "I loved the man he was before his obsession with magic consumed him."

"I don't want to turn into him."

"Then don't. Just be careful, Alexandre. Gaule is not ready for a king who does not bow down to tradition."

A knock rapped against the door and when the queen opened it, Anders entered, dragging a young girl by her arm. Alex stood.

"What's the meaning of this?" he asked.

Anders shoved the girl forward, and she stumbled before righting herself. Instant recognition sparked in Alex. He's seen her at the tournament and again when the village was attacked.

"Tell him," Anders ordered.

"Sire," the girl stuttered, pushing curls out of her face. "I have information."

A warning blared in Alex's mind. He remembered exactly where he'd seen her and who she'd been with.

The girl raised her chin. "I want to trade it for my father."

"Where is your father?" the queen asked.

"The dungeons, my lady." She averted her eyes. "He's a... magic man. But he's a good man. Kind. He'd never hurt a soul. I swear it."

"What is this information?" Alex bent to meet her eyes.

The sorrow that filled her face was heart wrenching. Tears dripped from her lashes onto her cheeks before running down the expanse of her caramel skin. "There's a..." She hiccupped a sob. "A traitor in the palace."

He put his finger under her chin and tilted her face up to look at him. "Tell me."

"Etta."

The name sent the room spinning and he almost couldn't hear the rest of her words.

"She's the daughter of the man who killed the king."

He stumbled back as a wave of nausea rushed through him. Persinette Basile.

"Get her out of here," he growled to Anders.

As soon as they were gone, his mother grabbed his arm. "Alexandre."

He ripped his arm away as white-hot pain thudded through his skull. Only hours ago, he'd been hopelessly in love. He felt every ounce of love being ripped away, replaced by the burning embers of another betrayal.

He should have known. Should have recognized the girl who'd meant so much to him at one time. But she wasn't that girl anymore. Was she in on the murder of his father? Why was she even at the palace?

"She's plotting against me," he muttered.

"Alexandre, no," his mother said.

"Then why else would she be here? She should want to be far away from any of us after everything father did." He turned on his mother, his eyes widening as he took in her worried expression. Worried, not surprised. "You knew. You knew and yet you still begged me to trust her. You sent Tyson with her. The only thing that would please the Basiles is our downfall."

"Then why is she getting Tyson and Edmund to safety?"

He didn't respond as he turned from her to wrench the door open. He began to understand his father in that moment, because he knew what it felt like, being king, and realizing that the only way to rule was alone.

He called to the guards waiting for him in the hall, pointing to one of them. "The queen is not to leave her rooms. Her maids will bring her food here. Only they are allowed in. As of this moment, Catrine Durand is confined by my order."

His mother didn't speak another word as he marched away with his remaining guards.

"Sire," one of them said. "The search of the castle is complete."

He'd given them a rather large head start, but he'd never regretted it more. "Take a contingent of men and begin the search between here and the border of Bela." He swallowed hard. "The girl is your top priority. Her name is Persinette Basile, and she has been deceiving us for too long."

"And the others?" he asked.

"They are no threat. Do not arrest them." Alex stopped as a strange pain radiated in his chest. "She is the one I care about."

He hoped they let Edmund and Tyson get to safety. Their only crimes were in their birth.

Persinette was different. All the questions he'd had about her since the tournament suddenly had answers. But they were no longer about Etta, for that girl didn't exist. He'd fallen in love with someone who wasn't real.

His old friend Persinette was the one who'd betrayed him. He wanted to feel anger. He wanted to hate her. But all he felt was a hole where his heart had been, and the suffocating truths laid bare before him.

CHAPTER 26

"I sort of expected to see someone come after us by now." Etta winced as she bent to tie the laces of her boots.

Edmund glanced up from where he'd been scrubbing at his skin. Tyson created a warm pool of water for him and he was beginning to look like himself now that much of the grime was gone. "Don't jinx us, dear Persinette."

Etta straightened and turned to tighten the straps of Vérité's saddle. "Don't call me that."

"It's your name." His eyes narrowed as he reached back to tie his now wet hair away from his face. Thick blonde hair still covered his cheeks, but underneath it all, he was Edmund, the first person who had befriended her at the palace. Her partner in turning the tournament on its head, and in keeping Alex safe.

Etta lifted one shoulder in a shrug. "I haven't been that girl in a long time."

"But you are she. Whether you've changed or not. Whatever people call you. You are Persinette, daughter of Viktor Basile."

She flinched at her father's name. "The man who killed your king." She was thankful for her father's actions, but she knew he'd go down in history as nothing more than a king slayer.

Edmund got to his feet, still moving slowly in his weakened state. He crossed the distance between them until he was right in front of her. "No," he said lowly. "The man who protected our people."

She remained frozen as he walked by. *Our people*. It'd been so long since she had been around anyone that knew the truth. They shared a connection, and it eased some of the pain she was still feeling.

Tyson bounced toward them. "So, are we going to ignore the fact that Etta is the only living descendent of the royal line of Bela?"

It took everything she had to keep her voice steady. "It means nothing to be heir to a country that no longer exists."

A grin brightened his face. "See, that's where you're wrong. It does exist. Bela itself may be unoccupied, but aren't all of us magic folk descendants of Bela?"

"Or Dracon," she said grimly.

"My mother told me I'm Belaen." He stopped moving and dropped to one knee.

"What are you doing?"

Edmund stood behind Tyson, shaking with laughter.

Tyson only smirked. "You're my queen. What do you think I'm doing?"

"Tyson, a prince of Gaule doesn't kneel to anyone."

He spread his arms. "Then it's a good thing I'm not really a prince of Gaule."

Etta clutched her chest as another tremor hit her. Tyson jumped to his feet and grabbed her arm. "Are you going to be okay?"

"Stop asking me that. The answer isn't going to change." She walked toward the horses. "We should get moving."

Edmund was able to pull himself up this time. He'd grown stronger as she'd weakened. She barely managed to climb on behind him and then they were off.

They reached the farming district around noon and Etta was consumed by thoughts of Alex.

“Can you tell me about it?” Tyson asked her. “About magic.”

“What do you want to know?” She winced from the pain.

“Everything. I’ve never talked to anyone who had it before.”

She forced a smile though she felt as if her insides were being ripped to shreds. Tyson truly was an innocent in all of this. She supposed she had been too when her father explained it to her. She tried to recall his words. “No two people’s power manifests the same way. Some may seem similar, but there are always little differences.” She thought for a moment as he nodded eagerly.

Edmund jumped in before she could continue. “Most people’s power is quite weak actually.”

Etta nodded. “Some have the ability to do great things, but most can’t. That’s why it’s foolish for the people of Gaule to fear all magic. Take Edmund for example. The most he can do is push sounds on the wind or give you a slight breeze.” She pinched his side in jest.

He took the bait. “And Etta here can annoy you by making the weeds in your gardens grow.”

She laughed. “I seem to recall being able to trap you with my ‘weeds’ when we first met.”

He shrugged. “You got lucky. I wasn’t expecting the thief I was chasing to have magic. I would have beat you without it.”

“Like you bested me in the tournament?”

Tyson howled in laughter. “She kicked your ass.”

“Barely,” Edmund grumbled.

Etta laughed. “If you’d like, I can go drop you back in that dungeon.”

He twisted in his saddle to shoot her a grin. “Not a chance. I’ve heard the legends of what the last Basile descendant is supposed to be able to do and I’m not going to miss the show.”

“What will she do?” Tyson asked.

Edmund shot her a wink. “They have a power that can do battle with La Dame. That’s why I never considered Etta could be Persinette.” He lifted one shoulder. “Unless she plans to tie her up in weeds and hit her over the head with a tree branch or something.”

His back shook with laughter. Etta dug her fingers into his side and hid her own smile.

As they skirted the edge of a rural town, the noise they'd been dreading reached them. Horses. Many of them. They thundered down the road. Edmund kicked Vérité as Etta looked back.

"I count six," she yelled.

"Think we can outrun them?" he called back.

"Normally, I'd say Vérité could outrun anyone."

"But ..."

"He's carrying a double load."

Etta reached behind her and pulled her sword free. Her weakened hand could barely hold onto it. Vérité lurched forward, and she swayed in the saddle.

"Don't let go," Edmund yelled. "Promise me, Etta. We're in this together." She didn't respond. Instead, she looked to Tyson. As the soldiers grew closer, he jerked his hand back to shoot water into the horse's eyes, but his aim was off.

Etta held out her hand, feeling her magic begging to burst free. It crackled but then fizzled out.

"Dammit!" she yelled.

One of the guards raised a bow and fired. Tyson dodged the arrow deftly.

Edmund tried to whip up the air to prevent arrows from reaching them, but his magic failed him as well.

They were close. So close. If they reached Duchess Moreau's lands, she'd protect them. That was what Catrine told her.

Another arrow narrowly missed Vérité's flank. That was it. She knew what she had to do. She leaned in as close as she could to Edmund. "Get the boy to safety."

Edmund yelled a protest, but she didn't hear him as she threw herself from the horse, landing with such force, it knocked her out for a brief moment.

When she opened her eyes, everything hurt. She could barely lift her head to see Edmund and Tyson hesitating. "Go," she croaked. They couldn't have heard her, but they did as she wanted, leaving her in the dirt, surrounded by Gaule soldiers.

The soldiers let Edmund and Tyson go, a fact she found odd, until one walked forward and sneered down at her. "Hello, king slayer's daughter. You are under arrest by order of the crown."

Her head hit the ground with a thunk as she let it drop. They knew who she was.

"Are you going to kill me?" She had to know. If they killed her, Alex would die as well.

"We have orders to bring you in alive."

She was hauled over someone's shoulder and then draped across the back of a horse. None of it mattered to her as relief rushed through her veins. She was going back a prisoner, but at least the pain would end.

A thick fist flashed in front of her face before darkness overwhelmed her.

Etta came to as they rode past the outer gates of the castle. How long had she been asleep? Days, most likely. Her stomach attested to that fact as it lurched from emptiness.

The pain had faded away now that she was close to the king once more, but it left her weak still.

As her eyes took stock of the goings on inside the castle walls, she realized nothing had changed. But her whole world was now different. She didn't come through those gates as the king's protector. She came through as a prisoner, an enemy.

People threw jeers at her as they passed.

The once friendly faces were now twisted in rage.

None of it mattered to her. She'd lost. She hadn't broken the curse as she'd promised her father and now she'd never get the chance. Their family line ended with her.

But then, that meant so did the curse.

Etta raised her eyes as best she could as they neared the inner gates. Her tongue stuck to the roof of her mouth and sweat began to bead across her brow as she took in the sight. The king awaited them, surrounded by his personal guard.

They stood in formation around him as if they feared she'd make an attempt to harm him.

They didn't know she was too weak to use her magic.

They didn't know how intertwined their lives were. That hurting him would hurt her. That she loved him.

All they knew was that she was a Basile and a descendant of Bela. That was enough for them.

Her eyes drank in the sight of Alex. After these long days of pain, the curse no longer burned through her. It rejoiced at their nearness, like it was a living thing.

Alex stood tall, but as they neared, she noticed the pallor of his skin, the half-moon circles under his eyes. He'd been feeling it just as she had. His crown sat straight on his head, but it shifted as his body lurched forward involuntarily. He covered up the movement with a cough, but she'd seen.

Her cracked lips parted as she was dragged down from the horse and dropped to the ground. They tried to form his name, but only air escaped her.

The guards shifted as the king moved forward. A guard behind her grabbed her by the hair and jerked her head back so she was staring directly into the king's hard eyes. He had no smiles for her, or words of comfort. He bent to push up the leg of her loose pants, his hands searing into her. When they grazed the jagged scar, he ripped them away.

Breathing heavily for a moment, he glowered down at her, betrayal in his eyes. "Let the girl have her father, it's her. It's Persinette Basile."

And that was when she knew. She'd been given up, traded. *Maiya.*

The anger appeared in a flash before it was gone. Maiya did it for her father. At that moment, Etta probably would've done anything to have her father back as well.

That wasn't the betrayal that mattered.

Alex knew who she was. He knew she'd been lying even as she shared his bed.

A sob escaped her. "Alex."

He shook his head and bent to look directly into her eyes. "I am your king. Speak to me as such."

As he continued to look at her, uncertainty and something she almost mistook for sympathy entered his gaze. But love? That was gone.

He wiped a hand across his face and she watched his heart breaking in two, feeling the same pain in her chest.

"Etta," he whispered so softly she almost didn't hear it. Then, as if he hadn't said it, he straightened and pulled his cloak around him.

A drop of water hit her face as rain fell like the tears she refused to cry. The king and his men turned and marched toward the dry palace.

Etta managed to push herself off the ground. As she stood, she lifted her face to the sky, letting the rain wash away her regrets.

A guard wrapped his meaty hand around her arm as another followed. They pushed her toward the stairs that would take her to the dungeons, her new prison. She squared her shoulders and raised her chin, holding her head high against the oncoming captivity.

For she was Persinette Basile. Daughter of the king-slayer. Descendant of Bela. Heir to the Belaen throne. She was cursed, and the cursed always had greater battles to wage.

ACKNOWLEDGMENTS

Whew… I have been waiting to write this for a long time. Golden Curse was written a year before the release and it's been really hard keeping it under wraps.

So, this acknowledgments page is a special one. Have you ever done something that felt like your entire career was leading to that moment? Everything I have learned has led me here. So, first I need to thank my teachers. The authors who've taught me, learned with me, made every mistake in the book with me. My shrinks. My confidants. My tribe. You're the ones I've known since the very beginning of this hard journey and I honestly don't think I'd be doing this without you.

To my family who sticks with me on the good days and leaves me alone on the bad. I appreciate you. I love you.

All those who had a hand into making this book what it became. From my incredible beta team to my editor to the talented talented designer who created the most beautiful cover I've ever seen.

Last, I need to thank anyone who dares to pick up an indie book. It's not always easy finding new authors and I'm so glad you've found me. Reading isn't a solitary experience. I'm on the journey with you along with every other person who loves Alex and Etta. Never stop reading and letting it shape who we are.

www.ingramcontent.com/pod-product-compliance
Lightning Source LLC
Chambersburg PA
CBHW030528310726
48979CB00010B/1843/J

* 9 7 8 1 9 7 0 0 5 2 6 6 4 *